MW00883369

FORTUNE TELLERS

ALSO BY LISA GREENWALD

Absolutely, Positively Natty

The Friendship List Series

11 Before 12

12 Before 13

13 and Counting

13 and ¾

The TBH Series

TBH, This is SO Awkward

TBH, This May Be TMI

TBH, Too Much Drama

TBH, IDK What's Next

TBH, I Feel the Same

TBH, You Know What I Mean

TBH, No One Can EVER Know

TBH, I Don't Want to Say Good-bye

LISA GREENWALD

FORTUNE TELLERS

KATHERINE TEGEN BOOKS
An Imprint of HarperCollins Publishers

Katherine Tegen Books is an imprint of HarperCollins Publishers.

Fortune Tellers
Copyright © 2024 by Lisa Greenwald
All rights reserved. Printed in the United States of America.
No part of this book may be used or reproduced in any manner
whatsoever without written permission except in the case of
brief quotations embodied in critical articles and reviews. For
information address HarperCollins Children's Books, a division of
HarperCollins Publishers, 195 Broadway, New York, NY 10007.
www.harpercollinschildrens.com

Library of Congress Control Number: 2023943299
ISBN 978-0-06-325585-2

Typography by Molly Fehr
24 25 26 27 28 LBC 5 4 3 2 1

First Edition

For my newest niece, Lennie Juliet Greenwald: wishing you a lifetime of adventure, friendship, and magic.

PROLOGUE

Bea's apartment, third grade

"I WANT TO BE A fortune teller, like for my job one day," Nora said, curled up tight in the corner of Bea's top bunk bed. Nora, Bea, and Millie were all in pajamas with their teeth brushed, and soon it was going to be lights-out. Bea's parents were strict about bedtimes and stuff like that. Stricter than Nora's and Millie's parents, at least. "You know how you see those fortune teller places on the street? I want to do that!"

"Ooh, that's like the best job in the world," Bea said. "First of all, you'll get to make our *amazing* paper fortune tellers forever, and second of all, you're helping people!"

"Totally!" Millie said. "Can we do it together? I want to be a fortune teller, too!"

"But maybe one day you'll need to do more than just the paper ones," Bea explained. "You might need to, like, have a crystal ball or something. I don't know."

Bea was the most reasonable of the three of them, the quietest, most agreeable, the one who always followed the rules. The one who seemed way more like an adult than a kid. Her aunt had epilepsy and Bea had to watch out for her a lot, so it made her more responsible.

"Yeah, maybe, but no one can make fortune tellers as good as ours," Nora said defensively, her brown curls bouncing on her shoulders as she talked. "I mean, ours are for real the best."

"She's right," Millie said, lifting her eyebrows. "We have the neatest handwriting of anyone in our class. Plus all our special designs . . . and obviously no one else has *the* markers."

"Let's just make as many as we can now and hand them out to people and predict their futures." Nora widened her eyes. "Imagine if our fortunes really came true! Like for every single person!"

"That's what we're hoping for, Nora!" Millie teased her.

"Wait—remember how Ms. Redwick said that thing about raising money for school the other day?" Bea asked. "Like how we could come up with ideas?"

"Yeah," Millie replied. "We were gonna do the bake sale. My dad's gonna make those brownie Oreo cookie bars."

"But what if we sold the fortune tellers?" Bea asked. "And then we donated the money to school. I mean, all the kids want them anyway, sooo . . ."

"That's really smart, Bea," Nora said.

"I'm in." Millie smooshed herself close to Bea on the bungee chair. "Let's make a million! Let's start now."

"Okay, calm down, Mills." Bea smiled. "Let's do 999,999 tonight and then the last one tomorrow."

Millie, Nora, and Bea were in third grade at the Shire School on the Upper East Side of Manhattan. It sounded fancier than it was. Shire was way more hippie than fancy—the kind of place where no one got grades, kids could choose electives from as early as kindergarten, and there was a huge emphasis on the arts. Composting was a thing at Shire way before composting was a thing anywhere else.

The girls had all met at Shire on the first day of kindergarten and had been inseparable ever since.

Millie's dad was an apartment building super, Nora's was an electrician, and Bea's was a professor. It's not like any of them were superrich, definitely not. They weren't the stereotype of Upper East Side private school kids. But the Upper East Side was home.

Until it wasn't anymore.

Until a pandemic happened and life changed so fast and Shire's lower school fell apart and Nora's parents got divorced and a work opportunity in the country presented itself for Millie's dad. Until Bea's mom decided they really needed space for her sister to live with them.

Until moves had to happen and decisions had to be made.

Until the three of them had the kind of fight only fifth, soon-to-be-sixth graders can have.

And then all went their separate ways and never spoke again.

CHAPTER 1

Millie

WHEN MILLIE'S PARENTS TOLD HER they were moving to "the country" to take over operations at a lake cottage community, she was mad.

Very, very mad.

Millie was used to life in Manhattan, going downstairs in the elevator, saying goodbye to the doorman on the way out, getting a bacon, egg, and cheese at Super Deli & Market across the street.

On the surface, it may have seemed like her family had a glitzy life, but they really didn't. Millie's dad was the super of the building, and so Millie's family lived there for free in a small two-bedroom apartment on the second floor, next to the laundry room.

It definitely wasn't glitzy, but it was good. It was hers, and she didn't want to leave it.

But now she had been in "the country," as her parents called it, for a year, and she was still a little mad but not as much.

Today was their one-year anniversary of being there, and Millie wondered if someone could really stay *that* level of mad forever?

Probably not.

"Millie, a new family's coming today," her dad said, the screen door to the rental office slamming behind him.

Millie was sitting behind the desk, with her feet up on the counter in front of her. "Maybe take your feet down; it's not the most professional-looking," he added.

It's not the most professional-looking, she mouthed without making a sound, but then she did take her feet down and studied her toenails.

Millie knew that if Bea were there, she'd tell her she needed a pedicure stat, and then Bea would probably take out her Caboodle and all her nail polishes and start giving Millie one.

It sounded gross to Millie, and she knew she'd never touch someone else's feet. But Bea never minded that kind of thing. Millie sorta thought Bea kinda liked it. Not the actual feet, like in a podiatrist kind of way, but in the *let me step in and help without you asking* kind of way.

Millie couldn't believe how long it had been since she'd seen Bea and Nora. Since they were all together, all the time. Since they made paper fortune tellers and had sleepovers, all sharing one twin bed.

"Millie," her dad said. "You're hearing me, right?"

"Um. Yes." She smiled. "Sorry."

She actually wasn't hearing him. She wasn't hearing him at all.

"Great. Thanks for being sensitive and helpful." He grabbed a rake from the back closet. "Off to sort out this pine cone situation down the hill."

Millie had no idea what he'd said before the *you're hearing me* part, so she decided to simply be prepared for any and all things when the new family arrived.

She picked up her phone and started scrolling through random apps, feeling bored but antsy.

I wish I were anywhere else right now, she thought. *But if someone asked me where, I'd have no idea where I would pick.*

Sometimes, when she was feeling really sad and lonely and curious, too, of course, she looked up Bea and Nora on social media. She hated that she did it, and she never admitted it to anyone. And thankfully, she didn't do it as much as she used to. But at moments like this when there was nothing else for her to do, and she missed her old life in that achy kind of way that somehow seemed to creep up out of nowhere, she just had to.

Just as she was about to deep dive into Nora's profile, Millie heard the creak of the screen door opening, and so she shoved her phone into her shorts pocket as a family walked inside.

"Hi! Welcome to Sheffield Shores," she said, smiling and standing up, pulling her V-neck gray tee so it was even on both sides.

"Hello there," a man said, taking off his baseball cap for a second and putting it back on again. He was a young-looking dad, younger-looking than her dad at least, but that wasn't so hard. Millie thought her dad looked like an old man, even though she'd obviously never tell him that.

"How can I help?" Millie asked, and then looked down at the notebook her dad had left for her. "You're checking into cabin 36, correct? Don't worry, there are, um, actual adults running things here. I'm just helping out."

"It's a cabin?" one of the girls shrieked. She seemed to be maybe eight or nine. Around the age of Sabrina, Millie's sister. The other girl was only about four or five.

"Well, luxury cabin, sweetie." The mom smiled. "Right?"

"Oh yes. It'll feel like a house, I promise," Mille told them, wondering if she was overselling it just a tad. "I used to live in an apartment building in New York City and now I live here, and it feels like we have a huge house."

Okay, she was definitely overselling. Maybe this was too far beyond what her dad had meant by being sensitive or whatever it was he said before.

"Thanks very much." The mom leaned on the desk

while the two little girls fell down onto the blue couch by the window. The dad followed behind her, but it became clear to Millie pretty fast that the mom was the one who ran the show here.

"This is a lot for them," she whispered to Millie.

"Well, we're happy you're here." Millie smiled and handed her the keys for cabin 36. "It's straight up the hill to your left. If you have any questions, call the main office. Someone is here from eight to six every day, but you can also call after-hours and you'll be connected to one of my parents, probably my dad."

"Oh, so this is a family business?" the man asked.

Millie hesitated. "Well, we all help out. I mean, not my sister, she's too little, but I help, and my parents are in charge, of course."

Millie forced herself to stop talking.

The two adults nodded, maybe not looking the most confident Millie had ever seen people, but not the least, either.

"So yeah, feel free to drive straight up to the cabin, and you can park there. As you know, they're all furnished and stuff, and you have access to the lake. And it's pretty fun here." Millie paused. "People live here all year, but it still feels like a vacation, kind of. So yeah," she said again, feeling like a human version of the palm-to-the-face emoji. She didn't have any idea what she was saying.

"Thanks for your help, uh . . ." The lady looked at

Millie's name tag, attached to her shirt right above her boob. She decided that after they left, she'd move it to a less awkward spot. ". . . Millie."

"Yup, you got it."

"Come on, girls," the dad said. "Time to go."

"But I'm soooo tired," one of them whined.

"I'm more tired," the other said.

Finally the four of them left the office, and Millie slumped back down onto the desk chair. Maybe it wasn't the best look that a twelve-year-old was checking people in. They didn't seem concerned, but now that Millie took a second to think about it—how would her parents feel if they showed up at a hotel or something and a kid was working at the front desk?

Millie knew this was kind of her own fault, though, because she said she'd help out for the summer. Camp was such a nightmare last year, she refused to go back, but somehow this didn't feel like the right fit, either.

She wondered if there was a word for knowing that things weren't right and at the same time not knowing how to get them right again or what would even make them right?

Nora would know. Nora used to know so many obscure, random words in the English language because her grandma got her a book of them for her ninth birthday and she memorized the whole thing.

Nora would know exactly what to say to Millie right

now, just like how Bea would start giving her a pedicure.

That was probably the worst part of it all—Millie didn't know *where* she wanted to be, but she knew she wanted to be with her two best—ex-best—friends.

And she couldn't.

That was the ache she felt—it wasn't for a place or a time or a summer experience.

It was for Nora and Bea.

CHAPTER 2

Bea

"SO, LIKE, YOU'RE A BABYSITTER for a grown-up?" Sam asked Bea, sitting on the edge of the inflatable pool in a way that would probably pop it and destroy the whole thing.

"No, I just keep an eye on her while my mom's out." Bea turned away from Sam and shifted herself in the water, rolling her eyes in the other direction so her friend wouldn't see. Sam wasn't the nicest person, but she was all Bea had, and being alone would be worse.

At least, Bea thought it would be worse.

"It's kind of weird, Bea. No offense." Sam blew a gigantic bubble with her gum and it popped all over her face. Then she tried to use her tongue to get it all off and the whole thing was disgusting to watch.

"It's not weird. She's my aunt and she has epilepsy and

we moved here so she could live with us," Bea said, hating how defensive she sounded. "Let's just change the topic, okay?"

Sam shrugged. "But isn't that so annoying? Like having to do so much to help out?"

"Oh my goodness, Sam! Stop!" Bea yelled, shocking herself with the sudden outburst.

Sam blew a bubble again, but she was neater about it this time. "Whatever, Bea. You're, like, wound up so tight. It's summer and you're stuck at home and I hate to say it—this inflatable pool sucks. You're one of the only people with a backyard in Brooklyn and you can do so much more with it. Maybe get a landscaper?"

She didn't stop and Bea couldn't understand why. It was just criticism after criticism.

"I'm just saying, you're capable of making things better . . ."

Bea sat back against the edge of the pool. She needed Sam out of there. She needed to find a new friend before school started. Okay, yeah, she also needed a better pool.

Basically she needed everything to change. Immediately.

"Hi, Bea." Bea's mom came out to the backyard, brushing strands of red hair off her sweaty forehead. "All okay?" She paused. "Oh, hi, Sam."

"Hi," Sam replied, not looking up from her phone.

Bea's mom didn't like Sam. She'd made that abundantly clear. But again—Sam was all Bea had.

"All's been fine," her mom said, like they were in the middle of a conversation and she was replying to something. "One seizure, but the kind where she just zones out for a minute. She's taking a nap now." She shook her head. "The medicine makes her tired. I need to call Dr. Gundersen again. He never listens to me."

She walked away from them, still muttering to herself. Bea figured that was probably the most they'd talk all day.

Before moving to Brooklyn, Bea had thought that having Aunt Claire living with them would make things easier on her mom. That's how her parents pitched it to her twin brother, Danny, and to her, at least. But no. So far it was definitely not easier.

"Okay, so can we go do something now?" Sam asked. "Also, FYI, this bathing suit is riding all the way up my butt and it's the worst wedgie I've ever had."

"Sorry." Bea made a frowny face, trying to appear concerned. "What do you want to do?"

"Get a new bathing suit."

Bea rolled her eyes. "I mean, today. What do you want to do today?"

"Anything, Bea! Anything! I'm so bored." She got up from the now-smooshed-in side of the inflatable pool. "I'm going to change. Maybe I'll see your brother . . ." Sam did that creepy eyebrow wiggle and it made Bea feel 100 percent icky. She was pretty sure Sam had only become friends with her because she had a crush on Danny. It was sort of hard to have a twin who, for some unknown reason, everyone found cute.

But sad times for Sam because Danny had no interest in her. The thing was, Bea had a feeling Sam would try really hard to change his mind.

"Gross, Sam. Really, really gross."

Sam was the kind of girl who kissed a boy for the first time in fifth grade. She was almost thirteen, the oldest in the grade by a lot. She only wore crop tops that looked way more like bras than shirts.

Grossed out from watching Sam walk inside, picking her wedgie, Bea slid farther down into the water.

She knew she needed to find other friends.

Or get her old friends back.

One or the other.

But fast.

"Bye, Bea," Sam called out to her through the screen door a few moments later. "I need to go. My mom just found out I failed math."

"Oh. Yeah. Good luck with that," Bea yelled back.

"Way to be a caring friend," Sam said, and then laughed.

Guess Sam isn't exactly mad at me, Bea thought. *That's good.*

Maybe neither one of them was thrilled with the other one.

Bea went back inside and slumped over the kitchen table, trying to think of something to do with her day.

"What's her deal?" Danny asked, his head almost nose deep in a bowl of Honey Nut Cheerios.

"What do you mean?"

"Like, why are you friends with her?" he asked. "You're always in a bad mood after you hang out with her."

It was the first time Danny had ever asked Bea about a friend. They'd been living parallel lives since birth and he'd never commented on anything in this realm before.

"She's fine. I don't know." Bea shrugged.

"Bea." He finally looked up from his cereal. "Do you need one of those apps to make friends? FindFriends-NOW or whatever?"

"Stop, Danny. I don't need your jokes." Bea left him in the kitchen and trudged up the stairs to her room to change out of her bathing suit. She figured she should be happy to have more space and a yard, but none of it actually mattered since she didn't have anyone she cared about to use it with.

After she was in dry clothes, Bea slumped back on her bed and stared at her ceiling fan, squeezing her eyes tight. If she just prayed hard enough, maybe she could be back in her old life in Manhattan in their walk-up apartment with her friends around the corner. They'd make fortune tellers with the silliest fortunes possible and draw with chalk on the sidewalk.

I want to go back to that, Bea thought. *So, so badly.*

But no. When she opened her eyes, she was still there, in her room in Brooklyn: friendless, alone, hot, and mystified by it all.

It had been a year and she had figured she'd be in a better place by now. She thought she'd be adjusted, settled, maybe even with new friends who she felt comfortable and happy with.

A year should be enough time for that, but somehow it wasn't. Somehow Bea felt worse than she did last summer. Probably because when you're first in a new place, you have all these ideas in your head about what it's gonna be like. And you daydream about all the awesome stuff. And yeah, it's scary, but there's also a feeling of hope and possibility.

That can keep you going for a while.

Bea felt guilty for being mad that her mom was so focused on Aunt Claire that she often forgot about her and Danny, but she did blame her a tiny bit.

A few moments later, someone knocked on Bea's door and for a few seconds, she pretended to be asleep so they'd hopefully walk away and leave her alone. But then they knocked again, and she gave up pretending.

"Come in," she said.

"Want to come hang with Craig and me? He's meeting

up with the kids down the block and I think they're going for ices or something?" Danny asked, leaning against her doorframe.

"Mom made you ask me, right?" Bea stared at the ceiling fan, feeling even more sorry for herself.

After Danny didn't respond, Bea said, "Just admit Mom made you ask me."

"Yeah, she made me, but so what? Bea, chill out. Stop being so grumpy. We only have like a week of summer left."

"Don't remind me."

"Come on. I'm never gonna ask you again so might as well just come with me now." He threw a squishy ball at her head and she ducked so the ball slammed against the dresser before bouncing to the floor.

"Fine." Bea shrugged, her cheeks a hint of red, embarrassed her brother had to be forced to ask her to hang out with him.

Danny and Bea left the house, saying goodbye to their mom and Aunt Claire on the way out. They were at the table working on adult coloring books.

Mom actually looks peaceful, Bea thought.

Bea's whole body relaxed for a moment, but her mind wouldn't let herself stay there.

It won't last, she thought. *She'll be twisted up and anxious again in five minutes, probably.*

"Stop being so miz, Bea," Danny said again. "Sam's

your only friend because you're always sulking. No one else wants to be with you."

"Stop! You have no idea what I'm going through. I don't need your advice!" She shook her head. "Let's just walk in silence, k?"

"K." He paused. "For the record, I'm already regretting inviting you."

Without another word, Bea turned around and went home.

I'd rather be alone than with him, Bea thought as she walked. *I would rather be alone than with most people,* she realized. *Okay, things need to change. And quickly.*

CHAPTER 3

Nora

NORA HATED CHANGE. EVEN THOUGH none of the changes of the last few years were her fault, what bothered her the most was that there was nothing she could do about any of them.

At her dad's new place, she had her own room, but it was beige. All of it. Beige walls, beige quilt, even beige wall-to-wall carpet, and in a rental, carpet is just kind of gross. How many feet had walked on it? Were there stray toenails stuck in the fuzz?

Gross. Totally gross.

Nora's dad wasn't the kind of guy who'd be like, "Let's design your room! We can go to Home Depot and pick out any color paint you want!" No way. He was the opposite. He was the kind of guy who'd be like, "It's fine the way it is. No one spends that much time in their room, anyway."

In fact, that's exactly what he said. On multiple occasions. To Nora and to her little sister, Penelope, who truthfully didn't mind the room situation (or the wall-to-wall carpet) as much as Nora did.

Penelope was only eight and she still got excited about new things. Unlike Nora, who was eleven and was just all-around disgruntled—a vocabulary word from sixth grade that Nora was using *a lot* lately.

It wasn't all bad, though. Nora liked the suburbs—driving everywhere instead of walking, the backyards, all the kids on her mom's block who just knocked on each other's doors to go ride bikes together. It was neighborhood-y in a different way than the city and life just felt, like, calmer somehow.

Nora was in the backyard on the hammock at her mom's house. It was that time at the end of summer when all camps were over and nothing was going on and each day melted into the next. Her friends would be coming over soon and they'd walk together to the pizza place. She felt lucky that she'd been absorbed into a friend group, despite being a new kid in the sixth grade. And she reminded herself of that all the time. She had friends, and a CIT job at the local day camp that had gone pretty well. And a hammock.

Things weren't bad.

But they weren't great, either.

"Nor-Nor, we're here," her friend Jade sang, skipping

through the backyard and over to the hammock. "Guess what? Jeremy Neiderberg likes you. It's official."

"Stop!" Nora's cheeks turned red in an instant.

"We will not stop," Esme said, plopping onto the hammock next to Nora. "He's super cute, he has a million freckles, and he likes you and we're going to all have boyfriends this year. That's our goal."

Nora felt confused by this plan because she had never agreed to it, and they were only going into seventh grade and Nora wasn't even sure she wanted a boyfriend.

"My sister said this is the best age to have your first boyfriend," Esme continued.

"And Pia knows everything," Jade added. "She's really all of our big sister. We need to follow her lead."

"Uh-huh," Nora said, only half paying attention. Her mind wandered to wonder if she'd ever feel comfy with Esme and Jade. *Kinda thought it would've happened by now.*

"Nor-Nor, how are you not more excited?" Jade asked. "Jeremy is so cute and he likes you! No one likes Esme and me yet."

"Don't say it like that!" Esme shrieked. "We don't *know* who likes us yet!"

"Can we go eat now?" Nora asked, actually hungry but also wanting to change the topic. "I'm craving the BBQ chicken pizza at Nick's. Like seriously craving."

"Oh, yum." Esme typed out a quick text on her phone and then shoved it into her pocket. "K, yeah. Let's go."

The three of them walked to Nick's, Tressdale's beloved pizzeria. It only took Nora, Penelope, and their mom a few days of living there to hear about the famous BBQ chicken pizza with the crispy noodles on top and the fancy sodas.

"Guys, I've been living in Tressdale for a full year!" Nora exclaimed, always the one who cared about dates and anniversaries and kept track of that stuff. Nostalgia was practically her middle name. "Today is our one-year anniversary of moving here."

At the beginning, after Nora's parents got divorced and they first moved to the suburbs, every day felt like forever. She couldn't believe a whole year had passed.

"Really?" Jade smooshed up her face. "Feels longer."

"Feels shorter to me," Esme said, matter-of-fact. "Way shorter, actually."

The two of them argued back and forth about this and Nora zoned out. They were always arguing and it was always over the dumbest stuff.

"What did we even do before Nora came here?" Esme asked when they were almost at Nick's. "Like how did we even survive?"

"No clue," Jade said. "Seriously. We were way fashion challenged and really bored and if Nora didn't show up we'd probably still be friends with The Coopers. Ew."

"They're not so bad," Nora chimed in, still very confused about how there were three kids in the grade with the last name Cooper, none of them related to one another, and how at one point Jade and Esme were best friends with all of them, a total crew, and then suddenly, out of the blue, they were mortal enemies.

"You don't know them like we do," Esme said. "Anyway, we're happy you're here, Nor-Nor. You're one of us now; thank *goodness* you don't talk to your city friends anymore. I don't want to worry about you moving back, or missing them, or liking them better than you like us."

"Wow. Harsh, Es." Nora shook her head, scratching an itch at the edge of her nose. She didn't like to think about Bea and Millie. She *did* think about them, of course, but when they crept into her thoughts, she pushed them away. She wondered about them, how they were doing, but she promised herself she'd never Google, or look them up on social media. Her mom never mentioned their moms.

It was just sort of a thing that was over.

And she was okay with it. Well, mostly okay.

Nora went back and forth blaming herself for the whole fight.

Today was an it *wasn't my fault* day.

I mean, it was fair for me to be over the fortune tellers. And it was fair that I was invited to a party and Millie wasn't, she told herself. *Very fair.*

Jade, Nora, and Esme walked inside and ordered the

24

famous BBQ chicken pizza and three bottles of the Nick's fancy white cola.

"So, first of all, I still can't believe that back in the day, sixth grade used to be in the elementary school here," Esme said after burning her mouth on a bite of pizza. She never waited for it to cool. Never, ever. "And it used to be kind of awesome, because sixth graders got all these special privileges." Esme's mom grew up in Tressdale and now had some kind of government position. Not the mayor, something else. Nora wasn't really sure.

"That would have been cooler for us, to all rule the school together when Nora got here," Jade said. "But at least now we've had a year of middle school and we don't have to stress."

"Pia says no one should ever stress," Esme added. "Because people can sense it. If we act confident, we're set. That's all we need to do. Ever."

Nora nodded. She *wanted* to say that she was getting a little tired of the Pia pep talks. *I never signed up for Pia to be my mentor. . . .*

Back in the city, Millie was Nora's go-to mentor-like person. They were definitely a trio—Millie, Nora, and Bea—and they were all super close. But Millie was Nora's one hundred percent best friend—the one she called with little things and big things and the one she could trust with advice and ideas and, okay, sometimes schemes, too.

She and Millie had convinced their parents to let them camp out on the roof of Nora's building one night; they'd convinced the doorman to sneak them extra candy on Halloween; they'd even convinced the super to let them time how long it would take to throw a marble down the trash chute from the eighteenth floor all the way to the basement.

The thing that probably made her the saddest was that she'd let Millie down. That somehow Millie wasn't considered cool and Nora hadn't done anything about it.

Okay, Nora, stop thinking about this, she told herself. *You're in Tressdale, and you're part of the "popular" group, whatever that means, a boy likes you, and most important, you're eating really good pizza. That's what you need to focus on right now.*

Stop thinking about the old building and Manhattan and Millie.

She knew there was no point in wondering what it would be like if the pandemic hadn't happened, their school hadn't pretty much fallen apart, and they were starting seventh grade all together, the way they'd always expected they would.

Nope. No reason at all.

"Nor-Nor?" Esme asked. Nora kind of hated that Esme called her that, but she never spoke up about it. It was fine. Not a big deal.

"Yeah?" Nora looked up from her pizza and wiped the corners of her face with a napkin.

"I said—do you want to sleep over?"

Nora hesitated to answer. "Um, yeah, I mean, I have to go to my dad's tomorrow night so sometimes my mom likes me to be home the night before, but she'll probably be okay with it."

"So it's a yes?" Esme asked again. "I have big plans for us."

Nora widened her eyes. *Okay, I'm intrigued, and maybe the tiniest bit concerned*, she thought.

"Yes. It's a yes."

CHAPTER 4

Flashback—March of fourth grade

SHIRE SKATES—THE SCHOOL'S ANNUAL SKATING party—was a highlight of every school year. The school rented out the rink at Chelsea Piers, and everyone would schlep over there, all the way to the westernmost part of the city, at the end of the school day. Parents would volunteer to chaperone and order pizza and bring desserts and come up with a fabulous theme.

"OMG, polka dots is the best theme ever," Bea said to the others as they were having their afternoon snack together at Ruby's, the coffee shop across the street from the Shire School.

"I fully agree. But wait, so who's driving us?" Millie asked Nora and Bea.

"My mom is," Nora said. "Your mom is driving home."

"And my mom is taking Aunt Claire to a specialist

at Yale. This one seems like she could honestly be the answer to everything," Bea added.

"That's so good, Beaz." Millie draped an arm over her shoulder.

After their snack, the girls walked five blocks to where Nora's mom's car was parked, and they headed downtown and crosstown to the skating rink.

All the decorations were bright and colorful—polka dots everywhere. And there were four (four!) tables of desserts. Everything from doughnuts to cupcakes to cookies, homemade and store-bought. All delicious-looking.

They found a bench, took off their sneakers, laced up their skates, zipped up their coats, and stood up.

"Let's skate!" Nora said, grabbing Bea's and Millie's hands.

On the ice, they held hands the entire time as they skated around and around and around the rink. Some Shire kids zipped by them, and others hung on to the wall. Music played—Katy Perry and Taylor Swift, Van Morrison, the Beatles. Something for everyone, even the teachers and parents.

"Guess what?" Emmett Conrad asked as he skated by them and then stopped.

"What?" Nora did a quick twirl on the ice.

"My fortune came true! It said I'd beat my record for doing something cold."

"Your record?" Millie was confused. "Record for what?"

He shrugged. "Skating! It's cold, right? And last year I did the whole rink one time around in two minutes. This year: a minute thirty! My goal was to beat it! And it happened!"

"Wow." Nora beamed. She'd written that fortune! It seemed so silly and she thought it would encourage someone to do an ice cream eating contest.

"Of course it came true!" Millie smiled. "We are fortune tellers!"

"You really are. K. Gotta skate." Emmett gave them a thumbs-up. "Later."

Bea reached out to bring the other two into a wobbly hug. "We're magical people, my friends. Magical, magical people."

They pulled out of the hug and went back to skating, hand in hand, until it was time for pizza. And of course, dessert.

"Thanks for helping me out," Millie said after she finished chewing. "You two are way better skaters than me."

"Not really." Bea shrugged. "And of course we'd help you! Shire Skates wouldn't be Shire Skates if you weren't skating with us."

Millie's insides felt like warm apple pie.

Bea and Nora are the only two friends I'll ever need, she thought, making a silent pact with the universe that as long as she had them by her side, she'd be okay.

At the end of the night, they all piled into Millie's mom's car.

"Can we have a sleepover? Pleeeeeease?" Millie asked her mom.

"On a weeknight? Mills, not tonight. Okay?" Her mom briefly turned to look at them in the back seat while at a red light, and then looked back at the road.

"But tomorrow is parent/teacher conference day," Millie reminded her. "Shire Skates is always the night before conference day, remember? So . . . not really a normal weeknight!"

Her mom sighed. "Our conference is very early tomorrow morning, though. I promise a sleepover very soon! Promise!"

The girls looked at each other.

"We'll even share a bed!" Bea offered. "We'll all cram into Millie's bottom bunk, so it won't be extra work. You won't have to open the sofa bed or anything!"

Millie's mom thought about it for a moment.

"We just want to be together," Nora said. "Pleeeeease. Pretty pretty please. With sugar on top!"

Nora and Bea weren't her daughters, of course, but they often negotiated like they were.

"Your parents will be okay with this?" Millie's mom asked, but she knew the answer. Almost always, the moms gave in for sleepovers when it wasn't an actual school night.

"Yes! Yes! They will be! Yes!" Nora answered for both of them.

They got lucky with parking that night and found a street spot on the first loop looking. And then they all went to Millie's, and Nora and Bea called their moms, and a sleepover happened.

Each wearing different pairs of Millie's heart pajamas, they all snuggled tight in Millie's bottom bunk bed, exactly like they'd promised.

"Best night ever," Nora said before drifting off.

"Definitely," Bea replied with a yawn.

"I'm already excited for next year's skating party," Millie added. "I think I can convince my mom to get me a few skating lessons before then. . . ."

Guess I'm the last one awake, Millie thought after no one answered her. She stared at the bottom of the top bunk bed, where Millie's sister, Sabrina, was fast asleep right above them, deep sighed, and then exhaled.

No doubt about it: this was definitely the best night ever.

But that's pretty much how she felt about all her nights with Nora and Bea.

CHAPTER 5

Millie

ONE THING MILLIE HAD NEVER expected about her new life at Sheffield Shores was how many little kids would try to hang out with her. She figured she'd help out at the desk and sit and read, maybe go swimming in the lake sometimes, but other than that—she'd be on her own.

But nope.

All little kids all the time.

"What's your favorite condiment?" one of the new girls asked while drawing on her knee with a fine-tip pen.

"Ummmm." Millie closed her eyes tight, wondering how long that ink would take to come off the girl's knee. She prayed that when she opened her eyes, the girl would have moved on to someone or something else.

"I guess soy sauce," Millie said finally, almost defeated that she had to answer.

"You like sushi?" the girl asked. "It's raw fish. So gross. I can't believe people eat that."

"It's really good," Millie said, worn out. "Listen, Kel"—the girl's real name was Kelly, but she insisted everyone call her Kel—"I gotta finish some work or my dad's gonna get really mad. So can I catch you later?"

Kel frowned. "Noooo. I wanna stay."

"I know, I'm cool. How about this? Go have lunch and we can meet at the lake around two." Millie smiled. "Sound okay?"

"No. But fine."

"Or go find Sabrina. I'm sure she'd want to hang with you!" Millie's sister was a more age-appropriate friend for Kel.

"She doesn't!" Kel yelled, and threw herself on the floor. "Sabrina haaaates me!"

Millie deep sighed and tried to calm herself down or at least prevent herself from freaking out. She was not Kel's babysitter, she was not Kel's friend, and she didn't want to do any of this. She just wanted to read her book and watch endless online reels of dogs doing silly things.

"Kel, Sabrina loves you, and you're going to be in school together soon, so maybe you could try and really become good friends before that, ya know?" Millie didn't even know what she was saying. She just wanted Kel to leave. She just wanted to sit back in the chair and not talk to anyone for a few minutes.

"She loves me? Really?" Kel stood up, looking through the screen door like maybe Sabrina would appear.

"Yup. Definitely," Millie lied. "Go find her. She's probably making string bracelets by the lake. Tell her to make me one, k?"

"K! Bye, Millie!"

Millie felt a nanosecond of guilt that she'd lied about Sabrina loving Kel. But so what? They were nine years old—kids that age all liked each other enough, didn't they? Plus, the more time they spent together, the more they'd like each other, and then Kel would leave Millie alone.

Once Kel left, Millie turned to her phone. She allowed herself a once-a-week check-in on Nora's and Bea's socials. She had to limit herself because otherwise it got obsessive, checking a million times a day, and she got too jealous and started to feel too sorry for herself.

But once a week was fine. She'd find out what they were up to, and maybe they wouldn't even have posted, and then she could just move on with her day.

I don't know why I do this, Millie thought. It was sort of torture and made her miss them even more. *I need to stop but I also can't stop and also don't want to stop. Helllpppp.*

But, I mean, I also want to make sure they're okay, she reasoned with herself.

Bea hadn't posted in a few days, but she rarely posted at all. And when she did it was silly dances with that girl Sam she seemed to always be with. However, Sam

35

would just stick her tongue out and make faces while Bea danced. "There's no way they're besties," Millie decided.

Nora posted a lot. Too much, actually. And always with these two girls who thought they were just sooo cool, Millie could tell. And Nora seemed happy with them. Like she was enjoying suburban life too much. They were always making kissy faces and doing weird poses. Pretty often, Nora's head was out the top of a sunroof.

Could you really get more suburban than that?

Definitely not.

Millie slid her finger up and closed out of the apps. *Okay, done,* she decided. *They're fine. They seem happier than I am, but that's okay. I'll be happy one day, too. I know it.*

Bea had that girl Sam, and even though they were mismatched, at least she had one friend.

Nora had two girls who really seemed like besties.

But Millie had no one.

She was one hundred percent, completely alone.

She allowed herself three minutes to feel sorry for herself, and then stood up, did some stretches, sipped some water, and pushed it all aside. Enough was enough. She was here. There was nothing she could do about that.

Maybe seventh grade would be her year and she'd find her people and everything would start going in the right direction.

This was *her* time for things to finally work out.

"Mill!" her dad said, coming into the office, putting

down a bucket and a soggy mop, and wiping some sweat off his face with the sleeve of his T-shirt.

Gross, Millie thought. Her dad was always too sweaty.

"Hi, Dad," she said. "What's up?"

"Another new family will be here in about fifteen minutes, so keep an eye out." He smiled. "And just in case I haven't made this clear: I appreciate your help."

He was gone before she had a chance to ask any questions about the family, so she figured she'd just sort of daydream about them until they arrived. It was a good way to pass the time.

Maybe they'd be from somewhere cool like San Francisco and they'd have a really cute son. Millie had never had a boyfriend. Not like a romantic boyfriend, which of course she'd never had because she was twelve, but not even a boy friend, like friend who's a boy. She couldn't remember the last time she'd had a conversation with a boy.

Millie propped up the little handheld mirror on the desk and inspected her face. Was she pretty? Maybe. Not the prettiest girl ever to live, but she was fine. Her freckles were in full force from the summer sun and her reddish-brown hair was leaning more toward reddish than brown. She didn't hate it.

Has anyone ever felt completely pleased with their appearance? Millie wondered. Maybe Nora, based on the zillions of selfies she posted, plus people always seemed to comment on how beautiful she was.

"Hello!" a woman sang, bursting through the door of the rental office. "We are so happy to be here! What a schlep!"

"And we're happy to have you here!" Millie chirped back, trying as hard as possible to match this lady's level of enthusiasm. Millie didn't have much experience in customer service, obviously, but she figured that was an important part of it—making people feel at home and welcome and like everyone was glad to see them.

Maybe that's the secret to life, Millie thought. *Making everyone feel like you're happy to see them.*

A few steps behind the mom was a boy.

Did someone just read my mind and manifest this real human boy to appear in front of me? Millie asked herself, lightly pinching her knee because for a second she thought she was dreaming, still lost in the scenario she'd been imagining earlier.

I am not dreaming, she told herself. *There is a boy my age here, moving into one of the cabins a week before seventh grade.*

An actual boy!

"We have three sons," the woman said, leaning over the counter filling out the paperwork. "Only one is here with us now, the baby of the family. The other two are still in Boston helping my brother with his auto parts company." She shook her head. "Oh, I don't know why I'm telling you this. . . ."

She spoke with sort of a southern drawl, but only a hint of it. Millie wasn't sure where they were from.

"I don't know, either," the boy said, finally speaking. He smiled with only one side of his mouth, and all of a sudden Millie wanted to know everything about him. She pictured them sitting side by side on the dock, their feet dangling into the lake, having one of those conversations where you don't even know what you're talking about but there's never a silent lull and before you know it, many hours have passed and you can't believe how late it is.

"What's your name?" Millie's voice came out crackly and unsure, but she was proud of herself for having the courage to ask. "I'm Millie."

"Rodge," he said. "Well, Roger, but no one calls me that."

"Cool. I'm Millicent but nobody calls me that, either, so I get it." She smiled and knew right then that they had an instant connection. Maybe it was only over nicknames, but it was something, and she was going to hold on to it. Millie wanted to tell everyone in the world about Rodge, but then she remembered she didn't have anyone to tell.

"Well, this is just lovely," the mom said. "I'm so glad Rodge has someone his age here. He was griping about it the whole ride!"

"Mom!" Rodge yelled. "Stop. Okay? Just stop."

Everyone stood there for a second until the mom finally asked, "And where would we get our keys . . . ?"

And then Millie jumped up, remembering that she was there to do a job. "Yes, the keys, right here!" She smiled. "You're going to drive up the hill and then it's cabin 518 all the way at the top. It's an amazing view, by the way."

"Thank you, dear," the mom said. "Roger, please come and help unload the bags. You know Dad's still having trouble with his knee."

"Yup. Coming." He sighed in a way that showed he was almost entirely out of energy. "Nice to meet you, Millie not Millicent. I'll see you around, or . . . ?"

"You'll definitely see me around, Rodge not Roger!" she said, her voice lifting at the end.

Okay, might need to tone it down a tad, Millie. You're coming across a little too enthusiastic, she thought.

Millie watched the mom and Rodge leave the office. She plopped herself down in the desk chair, suddenly sweaty and distracted, unable to remember what she'd been doing before they came in. Did she have any paperwork to file? Any phone messages to pass along to her dad?

She honestly had no idea.

It felt like today was the start of something, though.

For the first time in forever, Millie realized she felt hopeful!

What a feeling—enough to carry her through the entire day, maybe even the week.

CHAPTER 6

Flashback—December of third grade

"WE'VE BEEN HERE FOREVER ALREADY. Just pick something, Bea. Pleeeeease," Nora whined. "It's so unfair we're here in our favorite store and we can't even buy anything. I begged my mom to let me get something and she said no."

"My parents said no, too. It's so unfair," Millie added, stomping around the store. "I don't even know why we are here!"

"Because I never know what to get, and you guys got me this gift card so you need to help me! That's how it works," Bea answered matter-of-factly.

Millie and Nora looked at one another. They didn't agree. At all.

"Uh, guys, I feel like my mom wants to leave. She's looks really annoyed standing in front of the store," Nora said, looking through the big windows. "I don't know where your moms are."

"Okay, okay. Two more minutes," Bea said.

The girls wandered around Sticky Notes—their beloved neighborhood stationery store—stopping every other second to look at something new. It didn't matter how often they came in here, they always seemed to find items that were unexpected and exciting and that they absolutely needed immediately. Plus it smelled like butterscotch, and the walls were painted in light and hot-pink stripes.

"I found it!" Nora said, sounding excited. "How have we never seen these before? Oh my goodness. Come here!"

Bea and Millie hustled over to her.

"These markers. It's like they were made for us." Nora held up the pink, white, and purple striped plastic package with the curlicue font.

Millie folded her arms across her chest. "What's so special about them? They just look like markers to me."

She was still annoyed they were spending their afternoon helping Bea find a gift. She wanted to be able to get something herself, but her dad had said no every time she asked. "Bea has millions of markers."

"Look what they say!" Nora yelled, and a few other customers in Sticky Notes turned around.

Bea read, "*Write Your Destiny.*" She paused, wide-eyed. "Oh my goodness!"

"Right?" Nora rolled her lips together. "You need

them. We need them. Our fortune tellers need them! I can't believe we've just been using regular markers all this time. . . ." She shook her head. "These markers were made for fortune tellers!"

"She's right," Millie said. "You need these. We all need these."

Bea didn't say anything. She simply marched up to the register with the package of markers and her tiny little envelope with the plastic gift card inside.

After she paid for the *Write Your Destiny* markers, she had three dollars and seven cents left on the gift card.

The girls left the store and went back to Bea's apartment. They spent the rest of the day working on their fortune tellers.

From then on, those were their markers.

The only markers they ever used for the fortune tellers.

The markers that were literally writing people's destinies.

CHAPTER 7

Bea

THANK GOODNESS SAM IS AWAY this week, Bea thought while lounging in the backyard studying her chipping pedicure.

Was Sam on a trip with her grandparents? Maybe out east on Long Island? Bea couldn't remember. All she knew was that Sam wasn't here, so she could finally relax and breathe for a moment.

Bea wasn't sure what to do with all the hours and days of emptiness stretched out in front of her. As soon as she realized that, her stomach twisted up.

"Bea." Her mom came outside and found her stretched out on one of the lounges on the patio. "I'm taking Aunt Claire into Manhattan for a follow-up. I think this doctor's really going to be able to help us. I just have a good feeling about it. People usually wait months for an appointment with her but I got us in within a week!"

Bea nodded. She'd heard this so many times before.

I refuse to get my hopes up again. As far as she could tell, doctors mostly used guesswork to figure stuff out, and it seemed like most people were relying on miracles to stay healthy. "K, drive safe."

For as long as Bea could remember, her number one wish on all birthday cakes and pennies in fountains and eyelashes stuck to her skin was for Aunt Claire to be cured. It was pretty much all she wanted. Bea dreamed of Aunt Claire no longer having epilepsy, falling in love (in some daydreams, she'd fall in love with the doctor who cured her), getting married, having kids.

Bea wanted cousins. She wanted a big family where everyone went on a trip each summer and tie-dyed sweatshirts and sat around laughing about the same stories over and over again.

Sure, Bea had a twin brother, and they were sometimes close. Usually not, though. And a sibling wasn't the same as a cousin, anyway.

She wanted cousins who were her age, so that they could call themselves best-friend cousins like people did, having sleepovers and staying up all night on Thanksgiving, wearing matching pajamas.

It was too late for all that, though. Claire was in her midforties now and her epilepsy wasn't cured, and there was no way for Bea to have cousins who were her age.

Plus Aunt Claire's epilepsy pretty much consumed Bea's mom and the family. So wishing for anything to change didn't really make much sense. Bea needed to accept it for what it was and do the best she could to live with it.

It was gloomy, though, and sometimes Bea couldn't help but feel sorry for herself. Okay, she felt sorry for herself a lot. But she didn't want to. She wanted to change that.

"You okay, Bea?" her mom asked, but Bea knew better than to launch into a whole discussion about how she was feeling. Her mom was on her way out.

"Yup. Fine. Just relaxing."

"Love you, tell Danny where we went." She paused. "He's still asleep."

"Yup," Bea repeated. "Bye."

"Oh, and Bea?" her mom called back when she was halfway inside the house.

"Yeah?" She tried not to sound as exasperated as she felt.

"Try and clean up your room; school's starting soon . . ." Her mom paused. "I don't want to have to keep reminding you. It's not good to start a new school year with mess all over the place from the last one."

"K, I'll try."

She was grateful her mom didn't say anything else.

After that, Bea fell asleep on the lounge on the patio

and the hot August sun pounded on her cheeks so hard that when a notification on her phone pinged and woke her up, she was drenched in sweat.

"OMG what," she said aloud to the empty backyard, shocked she still had these notifications on. "Millie's posting on social media? What is happening right now?"

Bea wiped the sweat off her forehead and sat up. The sun was in her eyes, even with her sunglasses on, and she couldn't see so well. She got up and walked to the shade and clicked on the alert.

It was a photo of Millie's feet in a lake.

That was it.

Bea was suddenly overcome with jealousy even though she found lakes disgusting. But she was hot and alone. The thought of her feet in a crisp, cool lake almost felt appealing.

She stormed upstairs, fell back onto her bed, turned her ceiling fan onto the highest possible setting, and planned to stay there until her mom and Aunt Claire got home. There was nothing to do anyway.

But that only lasted so long. She felt more restless lying there, her thoughts spiraling around and around, and she couldn't stand it anymore.

Her mom was right.

About her room, at least.

Bea's desk—the top of it and the drawers—was a complete mess. Her mom was nagging her about it, which annoyed her, but the truth was, seventh grade was start-ing soon and Bea couldn't handle the thought of bringing home new schoolwork with all of last year's work still crowding everything.

Plus, she had to admit to herself—it was more than just this past year's schoolwork. There was so much paper jammed inside these drawers, probably spanning five years somehow. *I definitely should have cleaned this out earlier,* she thought. *Probably a dumb idea to move a desk from Manhattan to Brooklyn, completely stuffed up with paper.*

She walked over to her AC window unit and made it as cool as possible, pulled her hair up into the highest bun imaginable, and sat down cross-legged on the patch of pink rug in front of her desk.

Now or never, Bea.

This was the year she'd get organized, the year she'd figure stuff out—who she was, who she wanted to be, what she could control and what she couldn't.

Who knew attempting to clean out a desk would fill her with such purpose? Okay, she was getting ahead of herself. She hadn't even started yet.

First step was the top of the desk: a few workbooks, a math binder that was broken so pieces of paper were falling out, an award for perfect attendance, a permis-sion slip she never got signed to participate in some after-school chess club. Yeah, right. She was never going to play chess.

A note Sam had passed her in math class last year, saying she needed to stop being so emo and try to have fun. Okay, that was garbage.

Bea shook her head and then realized she didn't have anywhere to put all the trash. Her white wastebasket would never fit all of this.

She ran down to the kitchen to get a trash bag out from under the sink, and then trekked back upstairs, confused about how Danny was able to sleep so late, and went back to her desk-cleaning project. She turned on a Taylor Swift Essentials playlist on her phone and the music swirled around her room, somehow super loud even through her tiny little speaker.

She took it drawer by drawer—throwing away seemingly endless notes from Sam, all passed in class when they weren't supposed to be. The magic was that Sam never got in trouble. She was one of those people who appeared glowingly perfect to teachers, all smiley and polite, and then when they weren't looking—bam. Trouble.

Bea was almost done cleaning out the top drawer—most of it was garbage—but she found a friendship bracelet her counselor at day camp had made her three summers ago, so she saved that and a ceramic monkey she bought at a souvenir shop in Palm Beach, Florida, when they last visited her grandma. Then she found a few clumps of old Play-Doh—ew—she didn't have any idea when they were from, but as she hadn't used Play-Doh in the last five years, at least . . . wow.

Finally, she dug her hand way into the back to make sure it was all clear. She was going to get a paper towel and maybe some of that spray cleaner that her mom loved, and really finish the job.

And that's when she found it.

She gasped, shocked.

It was a fortune teller!

How is this possible? Bea wondered. *I threw all of these away after the fight. I know I did.*

She remembered doing it, too. So clearly. Ripping them into the tiniest little pieces, like confetti that landed all over the brown-and-pink rug in her old bedroom.

She used to have hundreds of them. Bea, Millie, and Nora were obsessed with making them in third grade. Actually, *obsessed* was an understatement. The fortune tellers were kind of all they talked about, all they did. They made them for each other, for their parents, siblings, classmates, teachers. They even came up with the idea of a fortune teller fundraiser and their school let them do it.

Their fortune teller obsession stretched into the fourth grade and then fifth, until, suddenly, maybe it wasn't cool to be obsessed with, or even to make, fortune tellers anymore.

Memories of that time flashed across Bea's brain,

aching like a broken bone that had never healed the right way.

Bea forced it all away. She refused to think about any of that anymore.

She held the fortune teller in her hand, scared and frozen. It was like she'd found something super creepy like human teeth or a trapdoor inside her closet. *These were all thrown away!* she screamed inside her head.

And now are they're reappearing!

WHAT IS GOING ON?

To be honest, she thought, *I kinda do need to use this fortune teller right now, though.*

First she picked a color—red—and then peeled it back for the number, opening and closing it six times after she landed on six, and then peeling back the paper to reveal her fortune.

Your future is hidden in your past.

What!

We never ever would have written this!

Her heart pounded and she threw the fortune teller across the room. It almost seemed like it was spying on her somehow or reading her mind. She looked around, suddenly suspicious there was a hidden camera in her room or something. Was Danny messing with her?

Frozen on the little patch of rug, Bea tried to calm

herself down. She breathed in and breathed out. Again and again.

"Okay, so," she talked out loud to herself, trying to figure out what was going on. "So a fortune teller I made in third grade that I'm sure I threw out is revealing a fortune that sums up pretty much everything I'm feeling right this minute? A fortune that wrote itself, maybe, because we never would've written something so serious. . . ."

She shook her head.

Whatever, Bea. Calm down. Just calm down and you'll figure this out.

"Bea?" Danny knocked after he'd opened her door a crack, which obviously removed the whole purpose of knocking, but he never seemed to understand that.

"Uh-huh," she answered.

"You okay? Are you having a séance or did you just see a ghost or something? I was calling your name for five minutes and you didn't answer."

"For five minutes? Really?"

"Yes. Want to come and get a bacon, egg, and cheese with me at Randolph's? And one of those giant iced coffees they wrap in aluminum foil?"

"It's weird that we drink coffee. You know that, right?"

Bea was talking to her brother with her back to him and she still felt pretty frozen on the rug. But the sound of a bacon, egg, and cheese and one of those giant iced coffees wrapped in tinfoil was way too good to pass up.

"It's not weird. Also, let's be honest—it's way more milk than coffee." Danny paused. "You coming or what? I'm starving. I haven't had breakfast."

"Danny, it's almost noon. Just call this lunch."

"Lunch. Whatever. Bea, you're annoying. Let's go."

Bea stood up and debated picking the fortune teller off the floor, like she needed to have it close to her because it was so freaky, but then she decided since it *was* so freaky, she needed to leave it there. Right where it was.

She abandoned her clean-up project for the moment, and hustled downstairs to meet Danny.

Before they'd moved to Brooklyn, Danny and Bea had tolerated each other, but they didn't really hang out or talk aside from regular family dinners and stuff. At Shire, they each had their friends, and they functioned in their own little bubbles that didn't really mix.

But when they moved to Kensington, deep into Brooklyn, and their entire lives turned upside down, they sort of had to stick together because that's all they had, and in a way Bea found that comforting. At least, Bea found some comfort in Danny. And Danny invited Bea to do stuff, so she reasoned he must have felt somewhat the same as she did.

"Looks like you decided to finally do the cleanout Mom's been asking you to do since school ended," Danny said to Bea on the walk to Randolph's.

"Like you've started yours," she scoffed.

"Well, I don't have as much to do. I don't save every piece of paper ever given to me like you do," he said.

"I don't save everything," she said defensively. "Most things, yes. But not everything."

They stayed quiet for the rest of the walk, not in an awkward kind of way, but more in a deep in thought kind of way. It was true that Danny had made more friends at Prenner than Bea had, but that's because it was easier for boys to make friends. They didn't talk about real stuff. All they did was quote *Simpsons* episodes to each other.

"Hello! The usual for my favorite still-sort-of-new-to-Kensington twins?" Randolph smiled from behind the grill as Danny and Bea walked in. He was always friendly to them, and knew their order. Randolph's was a neighborhood staple and happened to have the best bacon, egg, and cheeses in the city. Bea felt lucky to live so close.

"Yup! Thanks!" Bea smiled.

They waited outside since it was such a tight space and Bea shuffled her Birkenstock-clad feet on the sidewalk. She couldn't stop moving and at the same time, she couldn't tell Danny what was making her so anxious.

"Bea! Stop!" he said. "What is with you? You're like a ball of stress. It's summer for a few more days. Chill out, bro."

"Don't call me *bro*," she said. "I am definitely not your *bro*."

He ignored that. "Seriously, though. What is with

you? If it's about Aunt Claire, chill. She's fine. If it's about Mom's obsession with Aunt Claire, also chill because it's been this way forever and it'll be this way for the rest of their lives."

"It's not about either of those things," Bea said softly.

"If it's about how your friend Sam sucks, okay. Find new friends."

"Stop, Danny. That's not helpful."

He shrugged and went back inside to get the sandwiches and the drinks, and by the time he came back out, Bea was sitting on the sidewalk, looking Nora up on social media for the millionth time.

"So that's what it is," Danny said, looking at her phone screen before she could lock it. "You're never gonna get over moving and leaving Shire, are you?"

"I *am* over it," Bea defended herself. "Plus it's only been a year."

"Longer, but okay." His voice softened a little, and they walked home, eating their sandwiches at the same time.

Bea sort of hoped the walk would take a while. She was nervous to get back to her room and get back to the cleanout and especially back to the fortune teller.

Of course, *that* was what was actually bugging her, but she was definitely not going to tell Danny that. *He already thinks I am way too obsessed with the past and all of that.*

They finally made it home, satisfyingly stuffed from their sandwiches, still sipping the giant iced coffees.

She sat back down on her square of rug and had an epiphany.

So there was a fortune that seemed to totally encapsulate exactly how she was feeling right then. It didn't make sense, but she needed to see the other fortunes to try to figure out what was happening. If they all somehow corresponded to her mood and feelings and current situation, then something was going on.

If it was just one, it was a fluke. She'd move on. She'd throw it away. She'd never think about it again.

Luckily for Bea, she had many more drawers to clean out.

CHAPTER 8

Nora

JEREMY AND NORA WERE HANGING out that night for the first time and Esme and Jade couldn't understand why she wasn't more excited about it.

"Going into seventh grade with a boyfriend is like a guarantee that you're going to have an amazing year," Jade said, braiding Nora's hair. "I don't understand why you're not getting this."

"I am, I guess." Nora admired herself in the mirror, with Jade behind her. She was also a little unsure why she wasn't more excited. Jeremy was cute and funny and they went to temple together and she'd heard his bar mitzvah was going to be pretty epic. His dad was some famous cardiologist and they could afford a huge party. But she wasn't sure why having a boyfriend was such a big deal. She wasn't even sure she wanted a boyfriend.

"You'll be invited to all of the bar and bat mitvzahs for sure," Esme said. "I think we will, too, though. Just FYI. Don't think you're, like, cooler than we are."

Nora laughed. "The thought didn't even cross my mind."

"K, good." Esme popped her gum. "JK."

"Also not JK, though," Jade said.

Conversations like this made Nora's head spin. What were they even talking about? Everything was so intense with them—different friend groups, boyfriends, popularity, epic bar mitzvahs. Sometimes Nora felt like she was going to break out in hives from all the drama.

"You're nervous. We can tell," Esme said, flat on her back on Nora's bed. She was staring at her phone and talking at the same time, and it was clear she was distracted but also trying to be kind of a good friend.

"I am, yeah," Nora admitted. "I mean, don't forget, I'm younger than you guys. I'm only eleven. November birthday."

"We know." Jade bulged her eyes out. "You're, like, obsessed with your birthday."

Nora's cheeks turned pink and she wanted to say she wasn't, but she *was* obsessed with her birthday. This past year at her new school when no one decorated her locker or brought in balloons, when her mom wasn't allowed to make her famous chocolate chip and M&M cookies and send them in—it all felt depressing.

At Shire, birthdays were a huge deal. They were celebrated in class, in the hallways, outside on the playground on the roof. Everyone sang, announcements were made over the loudspeaker, the birthday person skipped around the cafeteria as many times as the age they were turning, so many treats were eaten.

It was *a thing*.

"So what are you guys gonna plan for me this year, then?" Nora asked, almost amazed by how bold she sounded. *Proud of myself for speaking up*, she thought, reminding herself she had actually found friends in Tressdale, and could and should have a tiny bit of confidence now.

"Ummm," Jade said, tying a little elastic at the end of Nora's braid. "All-night rager at Esme's dad's? He wouldn't even notice. Right, Es?"

"Yes he would," Esme said flatly. "We're not doing that."

Esme didn't like when Jade made jokes about her dad's living situation or the fact that he was out a lot and left Esme home alone so often. Nora picked up on that early but somehow Jade never did, or maybe she just didn't care.

"So what's the plan now?" Esme asked, changing the subject. "Are we staying with Nor-Nor until she meets up with Jeremy or are we going home? It feels like we're sending her off on some elaborate mission."

Nora laughed. "Elaborate mission or BBQ chicken pizza at Nick's?"

"No!" Jade yelled. "You cannot get that. Way too garlicky and messy. The sauce always drips down your chin. Are you kidding? You cannot eat BBQ chicken pizza with a boy!"

Nora shuddered a little. "Um, okay. Noted!" She laughed to try and break the tension, but it didn't really work.

She wanted them to leave. They'd been at her house for hours and her room was a mess. Jade had tried on every single thing in her closet; Esme had eaten an entire variety bag of chips and more Starbursts than Nora could count and left the wrappers everywhere.

She needed a break, and some time to mentally prepare for pizza with Jeremy. Also time to figure out what kind of pizza was acceptable to eat with a boy. Maybe that was something she could Google.

"You guys can go," Nora said finally. "I feel like I need to, like, meditate or something, maybe, and I think I'm meeting him in like forty-five minutes, so . . ."

Esme and Jade looked at each other, communicating with their eyes in this way they often did and that Nora didn't really understand. As much as she was included in the trio, it was still mostly them, with her a little on the side. Was she the pickle on the side of a perfect cheeseburger with crispy waffle fries?

"Fine," Esme groaned. "I told my dad I'd go out to El

Torito with him, anyway. I got in trouble for always making plans with friends during 'his weekends.'"

"I guess I'll just go home and binge something," Jade said. "K, come on, Es. Let's at least walk home together. Nor, you have to call us as soon as you get home, k?"

Nora nodded.

One of her favorite things about Tressdale was how small it was and how they could all walk to each other's homes. In that way, it felt similar to Manhattan. She couldn't imagine having to be driven everywhere, without any independence or freedom at all.

As comfy as she felt, for the most part, it didn't feel right that she was about to go out somewhere with a boy without Millie and Bea knowing. For the millionth time, she picked up her phone, about to just call them and fix what had happened. Beg for forgiveness from Millie.

But then, again for the millionth time, she couldn't do it. It had been too long. They didn't want to hear from her; the whole thing was pretty much her fault, anyway.

She was sure they had moved on with their lives, and Shire was way far in the past for them. They probably never thought about it anymore.

She put her phone down, determined to find her favorite lip gloss, the one she'd lost at the end of school, and had been searching for on and off all summer.

Nora kept telling herself she must've lost it at school and to give up searching, but she couldn't. She loved this lip gloss. It was from Sunshine & Co, her favorite Upper East Side boutique, and she'd had it for almost three years, using it sparingly so she'd never run out.

She needed it for tonight. It was the perfect level of gloss without being sticky, a tiny pop of pink, and when she wore it, she felt like she could conquer the world somehow.

Nora retraced her steps, trying to remember the last time she'd used it, and every time, she pictured herself at her desk, working on the math review packet for the final exam.

She'd put it on, trying to soothe herself. Nora remembered that part, but it was foggy and also confusing. Like maybe she'd had an anxiety dream about the math final, and imagined herself putting on the lip gloss. Was that possible?

Nora glanced at the clock above her desk and saw she still had forty minutes before she had to meet Jeremy. She put on the first outfit and stared at herself in the mirror—black flowy shorts and a hot-pink tank top.

Ew.

Then jeans and a sparkly flowy top.

Hate this, too.

I hate every single outfit!

How is it possible to hate every single thing you own when yesterday all of it seemed fine and maybe even good?

She did this over and over again—until the contents of

her drawers and closet were all over the floor. And then finally did another inspection of her outfit in the full-length mirror on her closet door.

I can't change again.

This will have to do.

Cutoff shorts and a gray tank with her little black hoodie in case it got cold. It was fine.

Good enough.

She *had* to find the lip gloss now, though. She didn't want to go on this maybe-date without her beloved lip gloss.

As she furiously tore through all her desk drawers, throwing mostly everything on the floor while searching, Nora's heart pounded like her entire fate rested on if she found this lip gloss or not. She had no idea where this intensity was coming from, or why she felt this way.

She started throwing random paper in her wastebasket, and at that exact second, her mom knocked on the door.

"Nora?" she asked. "You okay?"

"Yup, totally fine. Just doing some reorganizing." She smiled. "I'm meeting a friend at Nick's in a half hour. I'm fine to walk over there."

Nora really didn't want her mom to ask any follow-up questions. Not about who she was meeting at Nick's, not about the mess on her floor, not about anything.

The less her mom asked, the better.

Nora's sister, Penelope, was the opposite. She told their mom everything. They snuggled constantly, and when Nora and Penelope were at their dad's, Penelope was homesick. Crying for their mom all the time.

"I'm taking Pen over to Lily's house, okay? I should be back in about twenty minutes." Her mom paused, waiting for Nora to respond, but Nora was still searching for the lip gloss. She was running out of time to find it. "Nor?"

"Yes, totally cool with me." Nora didn't look up.

"You sure you're okay?" her mom asked again.

"Yes!" Nora yelled. "I'm fine. Stop! Mom. Seriously."

Her mom shook her head and left the room, and then Nora started crying. Out of nowhere, pretty much. She hadn't been feeling sad, but the tears appeared, pouring out of her eyeballs uncontrollably.

What is happening?

She sat down at her vanity table and stared at herself in the mirror, wiping the tears away and blowing some air toward her eyes to get rid of the redness.

There was one more drawer to check for the lip gloss, and she felt sort of dumb that she hadn't thought of it until now. Her vanity drawer—a totally normal place to store a lip gloss.

She opened it slowly and sifted through some old carnival beads, a pile of hair ties, a few headbands, and then she reached her hand toward the back.

Yes! There it was!

The lip gloss.

But her hand landed on something else, too.

A piece of folded-up paper.

Holding it in her hands, Nora started shaking.

I don't think I've ever missed something so much in my whole entire life, she thought.

It wasn't one specific thing she was missing. It was all of it from her old life. It was everything.

She opened up the fortune teller, almost wishing it were some kind of time-travel device.

Take me to my room in Manhattan, she thought, *with Bea and Millie by my side. Take me back to all of that. Please, please, please.*

She wouldn't be going to Nick's with Jeremy, she wouldn't know Esme or Jade, she wouldn't have to worry about her birthday or how many bar and bat mitzvahs she'd be invited to.

She pulled back one flap, not really using the fortune teller the way it was intended, trying to skip ahead to see the actual fortune.

Her heart thumped a little at first, and then even more when she read the writing on the page.

Stop doubting yourself. You're awesome.

She read it three times, somehow convinced that it would change and morph into something else.

None of this made sense. She hadn't made a fortune teller in forever. She distinctly remembered ripping all of hers apart after the falling out between her, Bea, and Millie. Plus when they did make the fortune tellers, the fortunes were usually silly. *You'll eat pickles for dinner every night* was one of her favorites. Or *Taylor Swift will become your best friend.*

This fortune teller appeared out of nowhere, she thought, *and unclear how, but did that fortune somehow write itself?*

She had to tell someone, but of course the only people it even made sense to tell were Bea and Millie. And she couldn't.

Penelope appeared in her room. She guessed they were back already? Maybe they hadn't left yet. Nora didn't know. It felt like her head was a thousand pounds and was about to wobble off her body.

"Nor? You okay?" Penelope asked her.

"Mm-hmm."

"Sure?"

"Yes! I'm fine. Pen, stop."

Penelope shook her head. "Ugh, what is with you? Mom just wanted me to tell you we're heading out, and make sure you don't need anything!"

"I don't need anything!" Nora yelled, way louder than the situation required, and she knew that but still couldn't seem to control her emotions or the tone in her voice.

"Sheesh. Fine. Bye."

Penelope left the room and Nora fell back onto her

bed, clutching the fortune teller to her chest.

It was a lie that she didn't need anything. She needed some answers to all the questions swirling around in her brain.

Where did this fortune teller come from? And why is it appearing now?

Is this some kind of weird prank?

Magic?

A message I can't ignore?

All she was sure of was that she needed her friends most of all.

She needed Millie and Bea.

CHAPTER 9

Flashback—February of fifth grade

"HIIIIII, EVERYOOONEEEEE," QUINN AFISCH SANG, walking down the hallway, where all the fifth graders were sitting in front of their lockers.

Fifth grade was the last year of Shire's lower school and so it was a privilege that they all got to have their own space to hang their coat and backpack, with a door that closed, with a combination lock, unlike the open cubbies the kindergartners through fourth graders had.

Plus fifth graders got locker sessions once a week, when they could literally all hang out in front of them, decorate them, relax, read, draw, whatever. It was a time to unwind and, according to Shire, "take a moment to step away and appreciate being in the fifth grade."

"Wait, guys, do you like this one?" Millie tried to get

her friends' attention back. They seemed distracted, lost in thought.

Pay attention to the red balloons you're about to see! She read it aloud and showed them the paper.

"Millie!" Nora whisper-yelled. "I told you to stop bringing up the fortunes in the hallway! It's embarrassing."

Millie's skin prickled. It was, like, out of nowhere that Nora didn't want to do the fortune tellers anymore. Just last weekend, at a sleepover at Bea's, they'd made fifty in one night.

"What do you think, Beazie?" Millie turned to face her.

"It's fine," Bea muttered under her breath. "Also, you know you can just call me Bea sometimes, right?"

Bea got up and went to talk to her brother, Danny, and Millie folded the fortune teller and put it in her pocket. She felt covered in embarrassment, almost like she was drowning in it.

"Sooooo I need contact info for my birthday party," Quinn sang loud enough for everyone in the hallway to stop what they were doing and look up at her. "An epic Benihana dinner with a sleepover at my apartment after. Boys come to dinner. Girls-only sleepover, FYI."

All the fifth graders were in the hall, and there wasn't a single Shire student who didn't like Benihana. And Quinn had a big apartment—everyone knew that.

"I need yours, yours, not yours, yours, yours, not yours,

not yours, yours," Quinn said, and went on and on down the hallway, pointing to people.

Millie froze.

She was a "not yours," and Nora was a "yours," and Bea was at the end of the hallway, talking to Danny about something, so Millie couldn't even tell what Quinn said to her.

The bell rang a moment later and everyone got up and grabbed their stuff to go to class.

"I can't believe this," Millie whispered, leaning in close to Nora, holding back tears.

"It's just one party," Nora answered. "It's not like Quinn's your best friend."

"Nora!" Millie yelled, way too loud for the hallway. "You're saying that because she asked for your mom's email. She didn't ask for mine! Think about how I feel."

"Calm down, Millie." Nora shook her head. "Also, I told you a hundred times to stop with the fortune tellers in school. Everyone thinks it's weird now. Maybe that's why she didn't ask for yours, because you're obsessed with something so babyish!"

It was like suddenly Nora was completely repulsed by Millie. Like just because Quinn Afisch wanted Nora at a party, Nora was way cooler than anyone else.

A second later, Bea appeared and smooshed in between them. "Quinn's not sure how many people are coming. She told me I'm on the maybe list, but she still asked for my mom's info anyway." She shrugged.

"It's in the Shire handbook not to talk about birthday parties in school," Millie declared.

Nora bulged her eyes. "No one follows that, Millie. You always talk about your birthday in school."

"Only to the people I'm inviting when other people aren't around!" By that point Millie was actually crying and she couldn't hold it back anymore.

Bea put a hand on her shoulder. "Millie, come on. Don't cry here."

Nora rolled her eyes and looked away, and it seemed like she wanted to sink into a hole in the middle of the floor and disappear from this situation.

"Nora, can you at least ask Quinn if I can come and be on the maybe list? Like Bea is?" Millie asked through her sobs.

"Millie, I can't do that." Nora folded her arms across her chest. "I'm barely even friends with Quinn."

"But you were invited!" Millie wailed.

"I wish you wouldn't make such a big deal out of this," Bea said to Millie. "Calm down, okay?"

"Neither of you get how I feel!"

Millie stormed away and locked herself in the fourth stall in the bathroom on the third floor. She stayed there for a while, sobbing and sobbing.

The girls argued about it until the day of the party.

In the end, Bea got to go. Millie was mad at both of

them for not standing up for her, or admitting how mean it was that Quinn did what she did. Nora was mad that Bea wiggled her way into the party and made a whole scene about it when she got there, over the top about being included. Bea was mad that Millie was willing to break up the friendship over this. Nora was also mad that Millie thought it was all her fault.

Somehow they were all mad at each other for different reasons, all having to do with Quinn Afisch and her party. But maybe it was about more than that.

Then, a few days after Quinn's party, the pandemic started and the Shire School went remote.

By then, Bea, Millie, and Nora weren't speaking to each other anymore.

Soon, they all moved away. Shire's lower school never reopened.

It seemed like all of a sudden their friendship magic evaporated, and none of them had a clue what to do about it.

* * *

From: The Shire School
To: Current Families, Past Families, Alumni, Board Members
Subject: Day to discuss Shire's future

Dear Friends of Shire,
Summer is quickly coming to an end and we are

looking ahead to a new school year. Please come to Shire at 11 a.m. on Wednesday, August 25 to learn about our plans for the future. Children ages 5 and up are welcome—childcare will be provided and much fun will be had on the roof.

Bring a bagged lunch and all the optimism you can muster!

Lots of love,
The Shire School Administration

CHAPTER 10

Millie

IT TURNED OUT THAT TELLING Kel that Sabrina loved her changed the whole course of their relationship. After that, Kel stopped bothering Millie, and Sabrina stopped whining that she was bored, and it was kind of a match made in heaven for the two younger girls. Which meant Millie had time to herself again.

Millie's mom was always talking about "manifesting." Maybe sometimes life was like that—you could manifest a situation that you wanted, or maybe just make someone believe something and then that thing would ultimately come true.

Like right now, she was about to finish her workday in the rental office, and she was trying to imagine a scenario where Rodge was waiting for her outside, and they could go for a walk together and sit by the lake. Starting the school year with a new friend would totally give her the confidence she needed to approach seventh grade.

This was going to be the year that changed everything, Millie decided. She then said those exact words aloud in a very quiet voice, as if she was putting it out into the universe.

"Mills," her dad said, coming in. "Just wanted to let you know I think Rodge's family will be here for the whole school year. So if you could make sure you're kind to him, and help him settle in, that would be great. Maybe tell him about Sheff Middle, stuff like that."

"Sure," Millie said, finishing her three thousandth game of Candy Crush. She tried not to appear too excited, because the vibe that felt most natural to her was never appearing too excited. But this time—she actually was.

She now had an excuse to be over-the-top welcoming to Rodge! Her dad had told her to. So even if she appeared overeager, it was okay, because it was kind of part of the job. It *was* part of the job!

"Thanks again, Mills," her dad said. "You know we couldn't do this without you, right?"

"Mm-hmm." She'd heard it so many times that it had sort of lost its meaning. They probably could do it without her, but she never said that.

"I think Kel's here for the year, too," Millie said, looking down the roster of families that were currently checked into a rental cottage, and noting what it said under *length of stay*.

"They are." He nodded and then opened his mouth like he was about to say more but stopped himself. Millie had no clue what that was about. She figured she'd find out eventually. It was cool how Sheffield Shores was evolving into a year-rounder community from a mostly summer one.

"So, anyway, you're clocking out, Mills." Her dad smiled. "Go have fun. Mom has book club tonight and Sabrina says she's sleeping at Kel's, so grab some leftover chicken in the fridge, or reheat a slice of frozen pizza. You're free!"

"Nice!" Millie smiled. Leftover chicken in the fridge sounded good to her, and she was kind of grateful for a free night. They were big on *a family that eats together, stays together* and sometimes it got to be a little much.

"Oh, and an email came from Shire—something about a meeting to discuss its future, I think." Her dad looked perplexed. "Have you heard any rumblings?"

She lifted her eyebrows; how would she have heard any rumblings? Her best friends for life had turned on her, and then they all moved away.

"Nope. Nothing." She wanted to know more. Of course she did. But she wasn't going to let the curiosity get in the way of her free night.

Okay, so my plan for the night: I'll go home, shower, eat

leftover fried chicken, walk around and see if Rodge is outside, try and talk to him . . . fall in love?

Millie laughed at herself but felt hopeful about the plan nonetheless.

She showered and was lying on her bed in a towel staring at her phone, one of her favorite things to do, when her mom barged in, carrying a giant box.

Wasn't she supposed to be at book club? "Mom, hello, knock much?"

"Sorry, sorry." She shook her head. "I'm on my way to Misty's for book club and I've been trying to organize all day. This is a box of stuff you might want to keep? Might want to toss? I'm not sure." She paused. "Please just do something with it. I'm almost done getting unpacked here . . . it's only taken a year."

Millie's mom chuckled and set the box down next to the window. "Okay, I'm off. I'll probably be home late. See you in the morning, lovie."

"Wait, um, Mom?" Millie called out.

"Mm-hmm?"

"Dad mentioned some email from Shire? Something about its future or, um . . ."

Her mom leaned against the doorframe. "Yeah, I'm not sure what's going on exactly, but I don't think we'll be able to make it to the city on a weekday. . . ."

"Oh, um, yeah." Millie nodded.

Millie's mom left her bedroom, and then the cottage.

The screen door screeched in the absolute worst way, and even though Millie's dad was perfectly capable of fixing it, he never seemed to make the time.

He was always fixing everyone *else's* stuff, Millie reasoned.

This giant box of who-knows-what was really getting in the way of Millie's plans for her free night.

Should she open it now? Or later?

Curiosity got the best of her, and she pulled back the flaps of the cardboard box and peered inside. So far it was just a bunch of paper.

She picked up her social studies binder from her last year at Shire. She opened it and saw all her old doodles: hearts and stars and rainbows.

MB + NC + BG = BFFFFFFFFF

It made her heart sting. So many forevers. All of them were a lie.

She tossed the binder aside and kept going through the box: every gymnastics certificate she'd ever gotten, and she didn't feel the need to save any of them since she'd quit gymnastics when they left the city. A red headband from the time she was on the red team at Camp Settoga day camp. A clump of lanyard she'd never made into bracelets.

Okay, all of this was garbage.

Why did her mom think that there was a need to save any of it? There was no reason for any of this to even have been moved from the city to Sheffield Shores. It was probably labeled trash and got packed by mistake.

Millie kept digging through the box: more random headbands and stuff, some bouncy balls from school fairs, a few drafts of a petition she, Nora, and Bea created to try to allow the kids to wear pajamas to school on Fridays. They didn't get very far with that.

Finally, at the very bottom of the box, was another scrunched-up piece of paper. Millie was about to add it to the pile of all the other garbage when she realized what it was.

Sure, it was scrunched up now, but back in the day, it wasn't scrunched up at all. It had an actual shape. Little slots in the paper where you could put your fingers in. Neat, crisp corners, words that were written in the neatest bubble letters possible.

Once upon a time, it was a fortune teller!

Millie stared at it. It felt like she was holding some kind of ancient relic in her hands—a reminder of who she used to be and the old life she missed so much. All of a sudden, Millie felt as if she was about to cry, scream, and laugh at the same time. Her body felt tense, holding every single emotion possible.

She burst into laughter, unable to really figure out which emotion was taking over.

Um, what is going on right now?

I know I threw all of these away after Nora told me they

weren't cool anymore. I know it for sure because I wanted to steal the matches that we use for birthday candles and burn them all, but I was scared I'd light the apartment on fire.

But actually, I could use a fortune, like, right now.

She wanted some kind of prediction—something to guide her when she was talking to Rodge, but also some pearls of wisdom for the school year.

Millie was determined for seventh grade to be great. She'd even settle for good. But at the very least, she wanted it to not suck as much as sixth grade had.

"Please, please, please let seventh grade not suck as much as sixth," she said aloud to her empty room.

She stared at the fortune teller in her hand again.

Some voice inside her kept saying, *Just open it, just open it*, and she couldn't avoid it anymore.

For something that had been such a huge deal in her life, Millie couldn't believe it felt so far in the past now, almost like she had dreamed it. Maybe she had blocked it out on purpose—the whole thing felt like someone poking her skin with the pointy edge of a nail clipper again and again. She knew she was the least cool member of the trio, but she'd never expected her friends to turn on her.

Millie went through all the motions of the fortune teller—picking the number and then the color and an animal drawing (Bea always did the drawings) and then going through the letters of that animal. In this case, a lion. And then she peeled back the corner of paper to reveal her fortune.

You are cooler than you think you are. Be confident! You rock!

She stared at the words on the paper. A drawing of a lion because Bea loved lions because of her August birthday. The bubble letters were all Nora. Hers were the best bubble letters of all of them.

Shivers crawled across Millie's body and she leaned over to grab her gray hoodie off her desk chair. She couldn't stand looking at this box anymore—especially since hearing about that Shire email—and she needed to get rid of it. She piled all the paper back in, with the fortune teller on top, and was about to lug it to the end of the driveway next to the huge trash cans.

But then she stopped herself.

She'd save the fortune teller. She had to.

It was a memento of who she used to be but not a happy one. It stung like the scrapes on her knees when she fell off her bike in Central Park in second grade.

But clearly, something was going on, messages sent from the universe maybe, and Millie couldn't throw it away until she figured out what was happening. Especially when it was exactly what she needed to hear at that very moment.

Millie dropped the box next to the trash cans, grabbed the fortune teller off the top, and pulled her hair back into a low ponytail. She'd forgotten all about the leftover fried chicken in the fridge and she was suddenly starving, yet too freaked out to go back inside her house.

Plus she wanted to find Rodge. He'd be at Sheffield Shores all year, and Millie was essentially part of the welcoming committee.

She'd ask Rodge if he wanted to go to Bear's Den with her, and she'd say she was starving and hadn't eaten dinner, and it would be the perfect place to go and a great way to introduce him to life at Sheffield Shores. They'd get chicken fingers and fries. And she'd get a Coke, too. Fountain soda was pretty much the answer to all life dilemmas.

Is inviting someone to get chicken fingers kind of like a date? The thought made her feel nervous to invite him. She didn't want it to seem like that. Not at all.

Millie walked along the path, past the storage shed where they kept extra lawn-care equipment and some abandoned kayaks. She walked up the hill, past the community gathering space where her mom sometimes had book club, and then around the corner past the dilapidated day camp building.

She was almost there, at Rodge's cabin, and her heart pounded. It pounded so loud she was about to turn around and forget the whole plan. She'd go back home, eat the leftover fried chicken, binge some show, and stare at her phone until it was time to go to bed.

That was pretty much how most of her nights went.

Filled with doubt and uncertainty, Millie convinced herself she couldn't do this. She didn't know how to talk to boys. She didn't know how to talk to anyone, anymore.

You are cooler than you think you are. Be confident! You rock!

The fortune spoke to her. Almost like a voice from deep inside her head, behind her ears, from some far-away place she'd never accessed before.

She *was* cool. She'd had friends once—good friends, too. Best friends. She felt cool at Shire, and fun and enthusiastic, up until the Quinn Afisch incident, at least. Until her friends had moved on from the fortune tellers without her.

This Sheffield Shores depressed version of Millie Block wasn't really who she was. She knew that. Her parents knew that. Everyone knew that.

"Millie!" She heard a voice and at first she thought it was that same fortune teller voice that was coming from inside her head. But then she heard it again.

It was a male voice.

And it was coming from up the hill.

"Millie!" he called again, and she looked up.

It was Rodge.

Her stomach grumbled and her mind went directly back to a Bear's Den plate of crispy chicken fingers and even crispier fries.

Forget self-doubt, all she could think about now was hunger.

"I was just going to Bear's Den for a snack," she said, not exactly yelling, but in a loud voice, as he got closer to her. "Want to come?" She stood up as straight as possible, smiling.

Way to not chicken out, Millie.

"Sure." He walked over to her, and then looked confused for a second. "Wait, what's Bear's Den?"

Millie laughed. She'd almost forgotten that he'd just gotten here that morning. She explained that it was Sheffield Shores' own little diner/coffee shop/snacky place, something along those lines.

They walked quietly down the hill until they got there.

You are cooler than you think you are. Be confident! You rock!

Millie kept seeing the fortune in her head and kept hearing some mystery voice repeating it to her.

She had no idea who'd written it or why this fortune teller appeared now, so many years later, but she decided she couldn't worry about any of that.

That fortune appeared for a reason. And it was going to take her places.

CHAPTER 11

Bea

BEA DECIDED HER MOM HAD been right this whole time—the chaos of her room was messing with her head, and that's why this fortune teller thing was bugging her so much.

Bea continued digging through her desk drawers—amazed and disgusted at the same time. *How did so many tubes of lip gloss leak?* Or maybe they'd melted onto the wood of her desk. Maybe the caps were never on properly. She went downstairs for some spray cleaner and some paper towels, praying that this was the right method to clean the lip gloss off.

It worked. For the most part.

She found exactly thirty-two hair elastics, which pretty much explained why she seemed to never have one—they were all in her desk. She hung them from the little switch on her lamp, worried for a second it could start a fire but hoping that it wouldn't.

Bea finally reached the last drawer—it was jammed and it took a few minutes to open it. One of her old writing journals was stuck. Then she realized there was a writing journal in that stack that didn't belong to her.

It was Franny Giles's, and Bea was tempted to read it, but then she decided not to.

At Shire, these reading journals were private, and Franny was kind of a secretive kid to begin with. Bea would have to find a way to get this back to her.

Now that most of the cleanout was done, Bea was excited to crawl back into bed with her old journals. Maybe they would help her get back on track and, like the fortune said, help her find her way.

At this point, anything was possible.

She opened the first one in the pile. It was from the very end of fifth grade.

A Poem on the Death of a Friendship
By Bea H. Grellick
Once best friends, now enemies
Once spent all the time together, now none
Once told them all my secrets, now my lips are sealed
Never expected this
Never wanted this
Now I am alone

Alone

Alone

Alone

Wow. Bea laughed at herself.

Wow. Wow. Wow. Fifth-grade Bea was really something, she thought. Probably even more dramatic than her about-to-be-in-seventh-grade self. Bea wasn't even sure how that was possible.

She turned the page and there was another poem. She didn't remember ever being this into poetry, but there was no denying it now.

Lost at Sea

By Bea H. Grellick

Without them, I am lost

I am lost in a forest of a million trees

I am lost in an ocean of a zillion boats

I am lost in my mind of too many thoughts to count

Without them, I am lost

Lost forever

No one will ever see me again

I will be here

But I will be invisible

She needed to stop reading yet somehow she couldn't stop herself. It all felt so painful, but not in that fresh it-just-happened kind of way. More in the discovering-an-old-scar kind of way and then touching it and then remembering how much it used to hurt.

Bea couldn't even piece together exactly what had happened.

Maybe it had ended up as one of those awkward trio friendships where one person always feels left out. But the thing was—in the beginning and for a long time, they were really all included and felt part of it, all having an equal role in the group.

Up until the end, Nora was more Millie's go-to person, but that was because Millie needed a go-to more than the others did. Aside from that they were fine: always having sleepovers at each other's houses, always doing everything together.

Then, suddenly, they weren't. And now they couldn't.

"Bea!" Danny pounded on her door.

She sat up in a fit, immediately assuming the worst. Aunt Claire had had a seizure somewhere; she'd passed out, hit her head. Mom had to rush her to the hospital. They'd be on their own for dinner. On and on. That's immediately where her mind went. That was always where her mind went.

Sometimes even worse places than that.

"What!" she screamed, and Danny burst into her room, falling onto her bungee chair and then bouncing up a little bit.

"Danny!" she yelled. "What is wrong with you? You scared me!"

"I know. That was the point." He cackled. "I'm just bored. What are you doing?"

"What does it look like I'm doing?" She rolled her eyes.

"Um, lying in your bed . . ."

"I was cleaning out!" Bea explained, frustrated. "I did my whole desk! Go look."

"Nah, I don't care." He stretched and put his arms behind his head. "Did you hear about this Shire email?"

"Huh?" Bea thought he was messing with her.

"Apparently everyone's invited to school to learn about Shire's future or something. . . ."

"Oh, um, that's . . . interesting." Bea's skin prickled. The fortune tellers showing up, this weird email, a chance to go back to Shire for a day?

It seemed like some imaginary power was forcing her to think about the past again.

"Anyway, Mom said we should order a pizza tonight. Aunt Claire's appointment ran late and there's gonna be traffic and blah blah blah . . ."

"Fine. Order whatever you want. I just need to finish this."

"Again, I'm not sure what"—he paused and then air-quoted the word—"this is. You're just lying in bed."

"Go. Now. And please don't sit like that—you're about to break my bungee chair."

Danny left Bea's room and she stayed in bed a little while longer, reading through her old writing journals. The Shire School was a place that was so focused on the arts they barely learned math, but writing was their main priority. She had at least six writing journals for each year she was there, and it was fascinating to pore over them. Almost like she couldn't get enough, like they were somehow a portal and she'd be able to travel back in time if she just read them extra closely.

By the time Bea had finished the last writing journal in the stack, her eyes were blurry and the pizza Danny had ordered was cold. Their dad was at a conference for the week and their mom was still not back from Aunt Claire's appointment.

She flipped to the last page, just in case there was something on the back cover. She didn't want to miss any of it. And then something fell out.

Another fortune teller.

Bea gasped.

It was opened up—just a flat piece of paper—so all the fortunes were visible to her right away.

That was cheating, of course; if she were to actually try to use one of these to predict her future, she'd have to go through the whole process.

But she was twelve years old and she didn't *really* believe in fortune tellers anymore.

Bea almost balled it up and was going to attempt to

throw it across the room into her wastebasket like a basketball star, but she stopped herself.

I can't just have them here and not read them. . . .

Revisiting the past helps us to see the future
Hold on to the memories
When all else fails, eat pizza

After Bea read the last one, she did ball up the fortune teller and throw it across the room, but she missed the wastebasket. She wasn't a basketball star.

And she was freaked out. One hundred percent completely freaked out.

These fortune tellers were somehow reading her mind, revealing her innermost thoughts. Sending messages about exactly what was going on in her life *right now.*

But they're written in third, maybe fourth grader handwriting, so how is this possible?

Those lopsided skinny letters written in purple marker were Millie's.

And no one in the world loved pizza more than Millie.

CHAPTER 12

Nora

NORA AND JEREMY SAT ACROSS from each other at Nick's, and all Nora could think about was Millie's third-grade birthday party at Pizzeria Uno on the Upper West Side. Everyone got to make their own pizzas and the party favor was a plastic plate in the shape of pizza slices. Nora still had hers in Tressdale. She used it pretty often.

Nora had this same exact thought whenever she ate pizza, and each instance felt new to her, like she'd just remembered it for the first time.

"Did you hear we're getting a pickleball option for gym this year?" Jeremy asked her after he burned his mouth on his first bite.

"No." She shook her head. "What is pickleball exactly, though?"

"It's kind of like tennis," he said. "But the ball is more like a wiffle ball."

Nora noticed he used the phrase *kind of* a lot and it made him cuter. She didn't like boys who were all full of themselves. Jeremy was a little more on the timid side, which made him seem nicer and more approachable.

"It's gonna be really fun," he continued, picking a crispy noodle off his slice of BBQ chicken pizza. "Did your old school have cool sports?"

Nora admired Jeremy's commitment to keeping the conversation going. Perhaps he hated awkward lulls as much as she did. Or maybe he was just really good at talking. Either way, it was a good thing.

"Not really. It was more of an artsy place. Like hippie-ish, I guess you could say?" Nora looked off into the distance, feeling those pangs of missing something so hard that you almost had to force yourself not to think about it. "We played volleyball sometimes. But one of our gym classes was guided meditation? If that gives you an idea."

"Wow. Yeah. That seems cool, though."

He also says cool a lot, she thought.

"Do you like Tressdale?" Jeremy finished his bottle of Coke and Nora could sense he had a burp coming on but was trying to ignore it.

"Um, yeah." Nora smiled. "I think so. I mean, my

93

parents got divorced before we moved here, so it's a little weird." She wasn't sure why she was telling him this. She figured maybe because she wanted to keep the conversation going, too, and so far she hadn't really said much.

"Yeah, that's hard." He scratched an itch below his left ear. "My parents are divorced, too."

"Really?" Her voice perked up and then she felt a little guilty about that. Like why should she be excited about someone having to suffer in the way that she did? But it was comforting, that's why. It wasn't that she was excited about it, but she was glad he could maybe understand her in this way, and glad that she wasn't alone in it.

"Yeah. Five years ago. My dad just left." He shrugged like he wasn't that bothered about it anymore. "Turns out he didn't want to be married?" Jeremy laughed, and he had one of those contagious laughs that made Nora start fully cracking up, even spitting some of her Sprite onto the plate in front of her, which only made them laugh more.

"Do you think that's why most people get divorced, though?" Nora asked, finally calmed down from the hysterics. "I mean, I guess they just, like, don't want to be married anymore?"

Jeremy bopped his head from side to side for a second, considering it. "Probably yeah, but there's also more to it, for sure. Right? I mean, what do I know?"

"Yeah, what do I know?" she repeated, and then they started laughing again.

I think this is the most I've laughed since I moved to Tressdale.

She couldn't believe how good it felt.

"So do both your parents live here?" Nora asked, finishing the last sips of her soda.

"My dad lives in West Crawford. It's like three towns away," Jeremy explained.

"Yeah, my mom is obsessed with a nail place there," Nora explained. "She tends to get obsessed with things. She's very loyal once she finds a place she likes."

Nora could see Jeremy getting bored. After all, most people didn't care this much about a nail place.

They finished their pizza and then Jeremy asked, "Want to walk around?"

Nora said yes, but she needed to use the bathroom first and then she felt super weird about that because even though everyone used the bathroom, it was still awkward to tell someone you were going to, and then did they picture you actually in there, like going through the things people do on a toilet?

The whole thing was super strange.

She peed and washed her hands and looked at herself in the mirror. Nora couldn't believe she was kind of on a date or whatever this was. More than that, she was kind of surprised about how well it was going, and how easy it was to talk to Jeremy. It felt better than talking to Esme and Jade. A lot better. Which was surprising.

She dried her hands on her shorts and then felt

something in her pocket.

Nora had forgotten she'd brought the fortune teller with her, convincing herself she needed it for moral support or something like that.

She didn't have a sense of how long she'd been in the bathroom, but a few more seconds wouldn't make a huge difference. She wanted another fortune, something to guide her for the rest of the maybe-date or whatever it was.

So she went through the motions super quickly, picking a number and then a color and then an animal and then revealing her fortune.

Sometimes the person you've been waiting for is right in front of you

She read it three times over and then looked around the bathroom, feeling like someone was spying on her again, or maybe Bea and Millie were right there, and somehow they'd written the fortune and then put the fortune teller in her pocket.

Her theories were all over the place and none of them made sense. She was frozen right then, in front of the bathroom mirror, looking up at herself and down at the fortune, and back and forth.

Then her phone vibrated in the pocket of her shorts.

You okay?

It was Jeremy.

Nora had no idea how long she'd been gone and she

felt more flustered than she'd ever felt in her entire life.

An email popped up at the same time; it was from her mom.

A day to learn about Shire's future was all she read before putting her phone back in her pocket.

She shoved the slip of paper into her other pocket and smoothed the sides of her hair and walked back out into Nick's.

These fortunes were supposed to help her, she figured, but they were messing with her head and making her even more confused and unsure about everything. And now this weird email her mom sent about *Shire?* Enough was enough.

This fortune teller was going directly into the trash when she got home.

If she was ever going to have a real chance of being happy in Tressdale, she had to get rid of the past.

CHAPTER 13

Millie

RODGE AND MILLIE SAT ACROSS from one another at Bear's Den. Even though they'd just met, they shared a plate of chicken fingers and a plate of fries—but got their own milkshakes, vanilla for Millie and chocolate for Rodge. Millie couldn't believe that she was actually sitting across the booth from a boy sharing food.

It felt like she was watching a movie of someone else's life, not her own, and that she was outside her own body. Millie kept feeling like the whole thing was going to crash and fall apart, so she didn't want to get her hopes up that Rodge was having fun or that anything like this would ever happen again.

Don't get too comfy, Millie. Don't want to jinx yourself.

"Like at Shire, for example." Millie was mid-story. "They did this thing where we'd have a parade each week.

It wasn't long or anything, just around the block. Some weeks it was a poem parade and we'd hold up a poem we wrote, sometimes a painting parade, sometimes with our instruments. One time we just paraded around with Popsicles." She paused. "You get the idea."

"Wow, that's really cool," Rodge said. "A Popsicle parade!"

"It was honestly the best place." Millie's throat got a little lumpy and she slurped down a few sips of her shake really fast.

"I don't get why it closed," Rodge commented, actually looking pretty gloomy about it.

"Well, not the whole school, just the lower school part. Kindergarten through fifth." She paused. "But I think it's because a lot of people moved away from the city during the pandemic, and then it just got really small and so they had to fire some of the faculty, and then more faculty left . . ." Millie wasn't sure why she was going into so many of the details about this.

"So you still keep in touch with your friends from there, though?" he asked.

Okay, so maybe he wasn't bored.

Millie hesitated to answer because if she talked about this, her throat would *really* get lumpy, and she didn't want to full-on sob in front of Rodge.

"That's a long story," she said. "Anyway, should we go? The lake is really pretty this time of night."

Rodge reached for a fry and then looked at the empty plate when his fingers touched only air. Millie had a feeling he expected to have at least one left. She knew that feeling.

"We have time. I mean, definitely enough time for long stories . . . ," Rodge said. "Well, at least until school starts."

Millie laughed for a second. "Yeah, I guess. But I've talked enough for one night. Tell me about you, and your old school and stuff like that. Well, we can talk while we walk."

Millie went up to the counter to pay the check, which really meant putting it on her parents' house account. Since they ran Sheffield Shores, they usually got snacks and meals at Bear's Den for free, but everything still went on the house account so they could keep track of it.

"Thanks, Sherman," Millie said, taking a wrapped red-and-white mint out of the little silver bowl.

"Welcome, Millie." He smiled. "Oh, did you leave this here?"

He slid a piece of paper across the counter. Well, it didn't really slide because it had corners and was sort of half standing up.

She took a step back.

A fortune teller. Here. At Bear's Den.

What is happening?

"Um, maybe it fell out of my pocket." Millie's cheeks felt fiery.

"Delilah loves those things. You should make some together one day," Sherman said. "Have a great night, Millie my dear."

Millie felt an overwhelming itch to just go home. She was unbelievably freaked out that a fortune teller had somehow appeared at Bear's Den when she was almost positive she hadn't even taken the one from earlier out of her house.

This had to belong to Delilah, Sherman's daughter. She was eight and the age of someone who would make fortune tellers and then carry them around with her and then accidentally leave them places. Millie decided she was getting spooked for no reason, definitely overthinking this.

No idea why Sherman would think it was hers.

She needed to go back to Rodge at the table, but she also needed to open the fortune teller and see if there were any clues inside about whose it was.

Do not ignore the signs in front of you

She clenched her teeth, folded the fortune teller, and put it into the back pocket of her jeans.

Nora's handwriting. No doubt.

"All good?" Rodge asked Millie when she got back to the table, sliding ten dollars across the table to her.

"Oh, you don't have to pay." She smiled. "We pretty

much get it for free. It's a long story."

Rodge laughed. "You seem to have a lot of long stories, did you know that?"

Millie laughed. "I guess I do."

They left Bear's Den and the fortune teller was still in Millie's pocket. She felt like she was hopping from one uneasy feeling to the next.

Someone was trying to tell her something, but she didn't know what, and she didn't know who, and she couldn't figure any of it out.

"Do weird things ever happen to you and you just can't explain them?" she asked Rodge and then instantly regretted it.

"Ummmm." He looked at her wide-eyed. "Go on. Seems like you're talking about some kind of sci-fi thing . . . I'm very into sci-fi."

"Well, not exactly sci-fi. I mean, maybe sci-fi?" She laughed at herself.

"Millie not Millicent—you're very mysterious, do you know that?" Rodge asked her.

"I'm not, though! I'm what people call . . ." She paused. "Basic? Uncool? I dunno, things just feel kinda weird at the moment. . . ."

"You're going to say it's a long story again. Aren't you?" He laughed.

They made it to the dock and sat down, dangling their feet into the not-cold-but-not-warm water.

It was silent then between them in an awkward way that seemed to sort of creep in the minute they sat down and put their feet in the lake. Millie was suddenly desperate to say anything and get the conversation back on track.

Even if this night had been perfect but then ended on a bad note, none of the before-stuff would make a difference.

"Did you ever make paper fortune tellers?" she asked Rodge. It was the only thing she could think of.

"Me personally?" he asked, sounding confused but also intrigued.

Millie nodded.

"No, but I know what you're talking about. They're cool." He looked at Millie for a moment and then back at the lake, still seeming confused and intrigued. "Why?"

She debated telling him the truth, but it was so weird and so out there, of course he'd be freaked out by it. But if she didn't tell him the truth, what would she tell him? It was such a random question to just ask out of the blue.

"My friends and I were obsessed with making them for a few years, like literally obsessed." She paused. "Anyway, I thought they were all thrown out years ago, but . . ." She hesitated to say the last part. "I keep finding them places today?"

Millie's voice went high at the end because even she was pretty unsure why and how she was finding these old fortune tellers, and she was also unsure why she was telling Rodge about it.

"Oh, that's kinda weird," he said. "Like you're going through some old stuff?"

"I was, yeah, but like Sherman at Bear's Den found one, too?" Her voice was still going high at the end. It all felt so uncertain.

"Mysterious," Rodge said. "And the one he found was definitely yours?"

She nodded.

Rodge said, "Well, one thing you might not know about me is that I'm really into mysteries, so . . ." He smiled. "Want to try and solve this one together?"

Millie's whole body felt like the moment before the Fourth of July fireworks started.

She wanted to soak in this feeling as long as possible, keep her feet dangling in the lake next to Rodge's.

Something was happening. And she was here for it.

CHAPTER 14

Bea

SAM WAS COMING BACK THAT night, so naturally Bea felt extra sorry for herself. And when she felt that way, she'd often deep dive into Shire's social media, deep dive into Millie's and Nora's, too, laze around and mope on her bed and try to imagine alternate scenarios where she wasn't living way out in Brooklyn with one terrible friend.

She was opening up Shire's Instagram to go back to the beginning, the first post, and look at all the photos when she heard her mom calling her name.

"Bea!" she yelled. "Come downstairs; something came for you!"

She couldn't imagine what could've come for her. Bea's mom was one hundred percent against ordering anything online. She hated the waste of packaging and she preferred to support local businesses. It was annoying and Bea couldn't wait until she was old enough to decide how to shop on her own.

"Bea! Hello? Stop ignoring me."

God, she always thinks that if someone doesn't respond right away, they're ignoring her. Sometimes people are in the middle of something or taking a shower or asleep.

Not everything is about you, Mom!

Bea trudged downstairs. Her mom and Aunt Claire were doing a crossword puzzle and her dad was marinating some salmon for dinner. Danny was eating a bowl of cereal and playing a video game at the same time.

"A box came from Shire," her mom said. "I followed up on that email they sent, and apparently they're cleaning everything out because they've finally decided to rent out the lower school classrooms to a local church."

"Really?" Bea asked.

"Yeah, without the lower school, they just don't need so many rooms, and they're trying to keep middle and upper open as long as they can." Her mom was able to do a crossword and have a full-on conversation at the same time, and it was pretty impressive.

"But who sent me the box?" Bea asked.

Aunt Claire was staring off into the distance, not focusing on the crossword puzzle. Bea knew she was going to have a seizure any moment and she was surprised her mom wasn't paying attention.

"Mom," Bea said.

"What?" Her mom looked up.

"Aunt Claire."

Bea's mom leaped up from the chair and went over and put her hands on Aunt Claire's shoulders, and then Aunt Claire started making gibberish sounds and moving her lips and tongue in weird directions and they all sort of stared, frozen in place even though they'd seen this happen so many times before.

Somehow it was still hard to go on with the moment when Aunt Claire was having a seizure. It was like time stopped for Aunt Claire, so time had to stop for all of them, too.

She came out of the seizure a minute or so later and then looked around, smiled, and went back to the crossword puzzle as if nothing had happened.

This was how it usually worked with her seizures, and this was a pretty mild one—nothing was broken, no one had fallen, her arms didn't need to be restrained.

The mostly silent, little-bit-of-gibberish ones were the easiest to handle.

"Momo?"

This was how Aunt Claire always came out of seizures. Momo was her nickname for Bea's mom. She'd made it up when she was a little girl and she couldn't say Molly and it had stuck all these years. Since Claire's and Molly's mom died when they were little, Bea's mom sort of became an unofficial mom to her little sister, Claire. And the relationship pretty much stayed that way forever.

Bea's mom and Aunt Claire went back to working on the crossword puzzle and her dad went back to the salmon and Danny went back to his cereal and the video game. No one seemed overly concerned or interested in the box, so Bea took it upstairs to her room.

Her first thought was wondering if Millie and Nora had received anything from Shire in the mail, and she had an achy feeling of needing to reach out to them immediately. She'd felt this way when she found the first fortune teller and after she heard about the email, too.

But now—maybe this box was the thing that would break up the silence between them? Maybe this box held the key to rekindling their friendship?

It was so weird because no one even really talked to Quinn Afisch before that party, or after. Bea didn't have a clue where she was now. *She's probably destroying friendships in a new town or a new school*, she thought.

We could have been nicer to Millie, though, Bea thought, her heart stinging. She and Nora had felt done with the fortune tellers, but Millie was still into them. They could have been gentler about it.

What it would it be like if all of that had been different? Literally all of it.

Bea was off on one of her imaginative daydreams again and she couldn't stop herself.

Sometimes her alternate scenarios were her happy place.

Bea started to open the box and the sound of a scissor slicing open some smooth packing tape was so delightful that Bea wondered why it wasn't an alarm-clock sound option on her phone. She opened the two side flaps of the box and then pulled out some old newspaper from the top. Underneath was a little envelope with the word *Bea* in pretty old-lady-looking handwriting.

Ms. Steinhauer.

She'd know that handwriting for the rest of her life. Bea tore open the envelope and read the note.

> *Dear Bea,*
>
> *Shire isn't the same without you and Danny. I'm cleaning out my classroom after thirty years and I stumbled upon this box of fortune tellers. I believe you, Millie, and Nora had intended to sell them all, perhaps? I think you did at one point. A fundraiser? My memory is foggy, but I knew right away that they were yours, and perhaps (most probably) treasures to you. I hope you're well. I hope you're reading as much as you can, and smiling, and finding all the joy you can in this upside-down world of ours.*
>
> *Please do stay in touch. Hope to see you at school at the upcoming event.*
>
> *All my warmest wishes,*
> *Ms. Steinhauer*

Bea started to cry.

Ms. Steinhauer was one of *those* teachers. The kind that everyone talked about years and years after they sat in her classroom. She was invited to everyone's bar and bat mitzvahs; students from thirty years ago would send her holiday cards every December. She was a Shire legend, a teacher who gave tours and spoke about the Shire School magic—the way that each and every student was loved and appreciated for who they were.

Bea read the note again and held it to her chest, like keeping it there would somehow bring Ms. Steinhauer close to her or make her appear or something like that.

Bea felt honored that Ms. Steinhauer had decided to send the box to her, and she was almost glad for a minute that she wasn't talking to Millie and Nora so she didn't have to share the fortune tellers with them.

But that feeling didn't last long.

Suddenly, all Bea felt was the complete opposite: the need to tell Millie and Nora everything right this second. She paced around her room, debating what to do.

Call them? Text? Read all the fortune tellers first?

Bea sat down on her bungee chair with a thud. Her body felt frozen, like fear was swirling around and around in her veins and it wouldn't ever stop. *The fortune tellers in my desk, the email, now this box—what is going on?*

She couldn't stop shaking.

She took six deep breaths.

She grabbed the top fortune teller on the pile.

Each section of paper was a different color. Bea remembered this phase. They'd had ideas to cover the fortune tellers completely in pastels. They were very into pastels. All pastels all the time.

Her heart pounded before she could even read it. Why was this freaking her out so much? She laughed for a second, realizing their third-grade selves would never have expected fortune tellers to show up like this.

They never would have expected to find them after all these years; never would have expected beloved Ms. Steinhauer to send a box of them home! To Bea's house in Kensington, Brooklyn! Not her beloved two-and-a-half bedroom, which was really a two-bedroom with the dining room converted into a room for Danny, on East Eighty-Third Street.

It was all so weird.

These fortune tellers were coming back into her life for a reason, but what was that reason?

Retrace your steps and remember what matters

Huh? We wrote that in the third grade? No way. These must be someone else's fortune tellers.

There was only one way to know.

They'd always put their initials in the corner in the tiniest handwriting possible.

BNM

It was theirs. But they definitely didn't write this!

And since Bea's initial was first, it meant that she made this one.

Her legs started shaking again.

This was the weirdest thing ever.

CHAPTER 15

Nora

NORA THREW THE FORTUNE TELLERS she'd found in the trash and vowed not to think about them again. At least that's what she told herself. But right then, as she was lying in bed, delaying getting up and starting the day, she regretted throwing them out.

She wanted some wisdom. And if the only place to get it was an old piece of paper from four years ago, maybe that was just how it was meant to be.

It didn't matter, though—they were all recycled; who knew what all that paper had been turned into.

Jeremy liked her. Esme and Jade were good friends, or at least good-enough friends. She was settling into Tressdale life and seventh grade was starting soon.

Time to be all in, Nora. Time to stop blaming yourself and put the past behind you. For real.

During sixth grade, Nora felt sort of half there. Or maybe, if she was being honest with herself, only a quarter there. The rest of her was still in Manhattan, missing her old apartment, where she couldn't even walk all the way around her bed, but it was the coziest room in the world, and more than that—she was missing Bea and Millie like she'd lost a limb. Maybe two limbs. Feeling the guiltiest any human being had ever felt; she was sure of it.

But seventh grade was going to be different.

Jade: I can't believe u wont tell us anything about you and Jeremy

Jade: why r u so secretive

Esme: jade, calm down. Stop being so jealous

Jade: ewww I'm not jealous

Nora: I'll tell u, I'll tell u

Nora: calm down

Nora: come over tonight—sushi?

Jade: YES

Esme: see you later

Esme: crispy rice here we come!!!!!

Jade and Esme (mostly Jade) were driving her nuts asking about Jeremy, and she hadn't really been in the mood to tell them about it. It just felt like a secret she wanted to keep for herself. Something about Jeremy texting her when she was in the bathroom to make sure she was okay felt special and kind, and Nora felt comfortable with him, like she could be herself.

She didn't really feel that way with Jade and Esme, but she'd never admit that. At least not to their faces.

Her phone buzzed on her night table, and she expected it to be another group text from Esme or Jade, but it was her mom.

Time to get up. Didn't want to yell. Come down and I'll make you blueberry pancakes. Love, Mom.

Nora laughed. Her mom knew not to sign her text messages but she did it anyway. And Nora appreciated that her mom wasn't the kind of person who would yell to wake someone up, and also that she was offering to make blueberry pancakes.

When she got downstairs, there was a plate of blueberry pancakes on the table, waiting for her. Her favorite syrup from their trip to Vermont last summer was out, along with a tall cup of fresh-squeezed orange juice.

Nora's skin prickled.

Am I imagining this or is bad news about to fall on me?

"Good morning, Norie-love." Her mom sat down at the table with her and folded her hands together.

"Morning, Mom." Nora eye-bulged, suddenly feeling nervous flops in her stomach. "Everything okay?"

"Yeah. I just, um, wanted to tell you." She paused. "Something came from Shire, and, um, I'm worried about giving it to you because I know how hard this move has been, and how much you miss the old days. . . ."

"What?" Nora's fork plunked down against the ceramic plate and a piece of it chipped off, but her mom didn't seem to care or notice. "What came from Shire? And how did they find this address?"

"I'm not sure," she replied in a weak tone.

"So why are you so nervous?" Nora asked. "Mom, you're freaking me out."

Nora's mom shook her head. "I don't know why I'm making a big deal out of this. You're happy here, right? It's better to have more space and you've found friends . . ." Her voice trailed off. "You probably won't understand this until you're a mom yourself, but I really agonized about this decision, and I guess I'm still agonizing about it, and so . . . I don't know what I'm saying."

Nora shoved a big triple-stack bite of pancakes into her mouth, mostly to avoid responding to this because her mom seemed all twisted up and Nora didn't know what was going on.

"So I'm not sure if I should give it to you, I guess is what I'm saying." Her mom paused again and finished the last sip of her coffee. "It actually arrived last week and then that email came. I've been avoiding dealing with all of this. . . ."

"Mom!" Nora yelled finally, when she couldn't take it anymore. "I'm fine! Just give it to me. You're freaking me out so much and this is not even a big deal. Why do you do this to yourself? And why do you do this to me?"

"Nora June Calzman, stop yelling."

They were silent then and her mom was holding her head, and Nora had no idea how this morning had gone from waking up slowly and lazing in bed to an offer of blueberry pancakes to being in a fight with her mom.

She wanted to start over.

"Mom," Nora said in her softest, quietest, most gentle tone. "Please just give it to me. I can handle it."

Nora's mom sat at the table for a few more seconds, not responding and not moving, but then she finally got up and went to the hall closet and came back with a small brown box. Nora's name was written in red block letters and the return address just said *The Shire School, Eighty-Seventh Street, NYC*. Then she sat back down and waited for Nora to open it.

Nora didn't know what to make of the fact that her mom was just sitting there, staring at her. She kind of wanted to be alone to discover what was in the box. But she was out of energy to have another almost-fight and curiosity was overwhelming her.

I need to know what's inside.

Nora grabbed her mom's keys off the hook and sliced open the tape. The first thing she found was a note.

Dear Nora,

I'm cleaning out my classroom after thirty years and I found piles and piles of these fortune tellers in one of the closets. I sent some to Bea as well but I don't have Millie's new address. Please pass some of them along to her. As soon as I found them, a smile appeared on my face thinking about the three of you and your boundless enthusiasm and creativity and zest for life. I miss you all terribly and I hope you're well, and reading, and finding as much joy as possible in this upside-down world of ours. Please send my very best wishes to your parents, and drop me a line to let me know how you're doing, if you get a moment. Maybe I'll see you at the upcoming event at school.

Warmest wishes,

Ms. Steinhauer

"It breaks my heart Penelope never got to have her," Nora's mom said, sniffling, on the verge of tears, after obviously reading the note upside down from across the table. "What a phenomenal educator."

Nora couldn't focus on any of that. There was too much other stuff in the note to focus on: the fact that Ms. Steinhauer had found them while cleaning out her classroom, that she'd sent Bea a box, too, and the fact that Millie didn't know any of this was going on.

Plus: Nora had a whole box of fortune tellers to read.

"Mom?" Nora looked across the table at her mother.

She was sobbing now. "Mom, what's wrong?"

Of course Nora knew what was wrong, but it still felt like something she had to ask.

"It was never supposed to be this way," her mom said, choking on her tears. "Shire was such magic. You were supposed to be there until you graduated. None of this needed to happen."

Nora deep sighed. They'd been through this so many times. Her mom never wanted to leave the city; she never wanted to be divorced. Nothing was settled; nothing was how it should be. The pandemic squashed all their dreams. On and on and on.

Ugh, Mom. I agree with you. But we have to move on. WE ALL HAVE TO MOVE ON.

Getting frustrated with herself, Nora stood up and grabbed the box off the table. "I'll be back soon," she told her mom. "Please stop torturing yourself. Okay?"

Her mom shook her head like Nora didn't understand, and before those exact words came out of her mouth, Nora's mom was alone at the table.

Upstairs in her room, Nora sprawled out on her bed and put her air conditioner on high. She was sweating out of control and her heart was racing and all of a sudden she was completely exhausted, as if she'd been awake for over twenty-four hours, even though she'd just woken up.

She quickly checked Bea's social media to see if she'd

posted anything about the fortune tellers or a box from Ms. Steinhauer at Shire, but nothing. Just a picture of her feet at the bottom of an inflatable pool.

But then again, was *she* going to post this? Probably not. So she wasn't sure why she expected Bea to post about it. But if neither of them did, how would they discuss what was going on? And how would she tell Millie? Would one of them reach out to the others? And who would be first?

She leaned back against her pillows, closed her eyes, and tilted her head toward the ceiling.

Nora needed to calm down before she could look through this box and before she could decide what to do about Millie. She wondered if Bea's note from Ms. Steinhauer had said the same thing. Maybe Millie and Bea had already reconnected. Maybe they were having a sleepover right now, discussing all this without her. Maybe Nora was already behind in the friendship restart. Maybe they would never be friends with Nora again, anyway, since she was the one who'd been invited to Quinn Afisch's party in the first place and then the one who'd made Millie feel bad about the fortune tellers.

Her mind twisted in every direction possible until she was too anxious to even stay in her bed and she had to get up and start walking around her room. She stared out the window at the elderly couple across the street having breakfast on their front porch. They seemed so peaceful and content and she wished that she felt that way.

"Mom wants to know if you're okay." Penelope burst into the room, a Tootsie Pop in the corner of her cheek, even though it was still morning. "She's dropping me off at the pool. Wanna come? She said she'd give us each ten dollars for lunch but I'm gonna get double ice cream and not tell her."

"I'm fine but not ready yet. I'll walk over and meet you later." Nora half smiled so Penelope would think she was fine and leave the room. "K?"

"Sure, whatever."

Penelope didn't really worry about stuff. She only seemed to care about whatever was directly in front of her. Nora wished she could be like that. It seemed so much easier.

Maybe that was the reason for the falling out. Or one of the reasons, anyway. Because she was too obsessed with fitting in with everyone. So that when she actually got invited to Quinn's party, she felt like she had to jump at the chance to go.

Had she been more like her younger sister, more outspoken, more comfortable in her own skin, she might still be friends with Millie and Bea.

Nora blamed herself. For most things. But especially this thing.

She paced around her room for a few more minutes until the box seemed to be staring at her from across the room, saying *open me, open me.*

"Nora!" her mom yelled from downstairs. It seemed she was done with the texting method of communication from one floor to another. "Taking Pen to the pool. Be back soon."

"K!" Nora yelled back.

For some reason Nora needed to hear the screen door close to be able to open the box. She needed privacy, she told herself. After all, it felt like she was opening some kind of secret door to her past and she wasn't sure what she'd discover or how she'd feel after she discovered it.

She took the first one out of the box and stared at it. Had she made this one? Had Millie? Had Bea? She couldn't tell. It was neatly written and Bea had the neatest handwriting of all of them, but Bea hated pink and this one was entirely covered in different shades of pink.

The four colors listed were teal, aqua, violet, and pink.

Such obscure colors. This was probably a Millie fortune teller.

Nora picked the color pink and moved the fortune teller.

P-I-N-K.

Then she picked the number eight and moved the fortune teller eight times.

Nora skipped ahead and pulled back the corner of the paper to reveal the fortune, but she closed her eyes before she read it, almost praying that it would be something good or helpful, at least.

Make peace with the past so you can crush your future

Her fingertips were sweating onto the paper while Nora read the fortune over and over again. It was written in scrawly third grader handwriting and definitely seemed way more mature than something they would have come up with back then.

But then Nora remembered where it came from.

Danny was obsessed with this video game where people designed their futures—everything from their homes to their jobs to their kids to the meal they cooked on a random Tuesday.

Make peace with the past so you can crush your future was the tagline for it, and one day the three of them were at Bea and Danny's apartment and he was playing it so intently that Bea, Millie, and Nora stood next to him and said it over and over again, just to be annoying.

He ended up throwing the controller across the room and cracking the TV screen and then Bea and Danny's dad got really mad and Nora and Millie ran home.

Guess it wasn't the nicest thing to repeat the same thing over and over again, trying super hard to annoy someone, Nora decided.

But now—the fact that this was coming back to haunt her. There was no doubt about it: she had to own up to her mistakes; she had to apologize to Millie.

She had to find Millie and Bea and reconnect and say she was sorry.

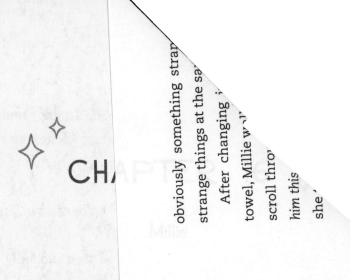

MILLIE WAS EATING BREAKFAST WHEN her dad made an announcement.

"Millie, I'm giving you the day off. It's Friday. School starts soon, and you've done enough work. Go have fun!"

"Um, okay." Millie smiled and knew she should probably feel more grateful for this, but all she could think about was that she had whole day off in front of her and couldn't come up with anything to do. Her mom got up to put some dishes in the dishwasher. "Okay, I'm off to the food pantry with Maureen. See you lovies later."

"Does Rodge's mom volunteer there?" Millie asked as her mom was almost out the door.

"Not exactly. Mills, I gotta run. We'll discuss later." She smiled. "Love you up to the moon."

Millie and Sabrina stared at each other. There was

ge going on. Like a million
me time.

nto a bathing suit and grabbing a
ked down to the lake. She'd lounge there,
n social media, and then text Rodge. *Texting*
arly in the day will be coming on wayyyyy too strong,
old herself.

She got down to the dock, about to dip her feet in, and saw him.

OMG. He's already here. Her stomach was suddenly a sheet of bubble wrap.

"Hey, Rodge! You're up early." She smiled.

"Yeah." There was something in his tone that sounded defeated. Way different from his whole "I like to solve mysteries" vibe from the other day.

"You okay?" Millie asked.

"Eh." He paused. "Can I ask you something?"

Her heart pounded and her anxiety seemed to shoot off the charts after that question.

No one ever feels comfy when asked that, she thought.

She nodded. "Of course."

"Are people nice at school here?"

"Ummm." She hesitated. "I'll be honest, I haven't really found my people here yet, but it's not that they're mean or anything. . . ."

Rodge was quiet after that and Millie scanned her

brain for some excuse to get up and leave. This wasn't the Rodge from the Bear's Den the other night and she wasn't sure what to do about it.

"I'm sure you've heard our story by now," Rodge said, untangling some seaweed off his foot. Millie couldn't look. She hated hated hated seaweed. Millie would take concrete and the overflowing garbage bags on the city streets over seaweed any day.

"I don't think I have actually," Millie said softly, trying to be open to whatever he was about to say and also make it clear people weren't gossiping about his family or anything.

"We're here because we were living below the poverty line," he said finally. "Whatever that means; I've heard my parents say it a million times and it's still confusing to me. Anyway, my mom applied for some grant." He looked at her, seeming frustrated that he had to spell this all out. "You don't need to pretend, Millie. Your mom is going with my mom to the food pantry today."

Millie's face felt prickly. She felt ashamed, too, assuming that they were going to volunteer when really her mom was going with Rodge's mom to pick up food. She wanted to run away and never see Rodge again.

"Oh, um, yeah. I just sort of heard that in passing," Millie said. "But, um, I didn't know the details, or . . ."

"You mean you've never known anyone who had to

shop at a food pantry?" he asked. "Or is it even considered shopping if you're just taking food?" He looked away.
"Whatever. I need to go."

Rodge got up and slipped his feet into his flip-flops,
threw his towel over his shoulders, and walked away.

Millie was frozen on the dock. The lake water felt icy
even though it was as warm as it would get.

She sat back, trying to think of what to do. Follow him?
Probably not. Maybe check in on him later? Probably yes.
She'd talk to her mom and figure out what the deal was
and get more info and then go from there.

Millie took her phone to text Rodge and at least say
she was here for him or something.

Her phone buzzed with a notification.

I was tagged in a photo?

Nora tagged me in a photo?!

It felt like her chest exploded then. Sort of in a good
way, but not really. More in shocked way.

These were the best, the caption said.

The photo was of a box and then six fortune tellers
standing up tall and even in front of it. Millie wondered
how long it had taken Nora to set this up so it would be
just so. Nora was a perfectionist in that way, and in most
ways. Because of that, her social media presence was
always sort of perfect.

Did this mean the fortune tellers were appearing again
for all of them? At least for Nora and Millie. But probably

for Bea, too. It couldn't just be two of them.

Millie clicked on the photo to see if anyone had commented yet.

No. So far only a few hearts.

She stared at it for what felt like hours, but truthfully it was only five minutes or so.

And she decided to comment.

Absolute best. Miss you.

She instantly regretted it. Why was she opening herself up to this? Especially after the whole Quinn Afisch incident, and how mean Nora was to her at the end about the fortune tellers, and then the pandemic happening and everyone moving away.

But it was too late to delete it because Nora had already responded.

Same.

CHAPTER 17

Bea

I JUST WANT TO HIDE under the covers and avoid the world, Bea thought.

Aunt Claire had had two tonic-clonic seizures last night—the kind where she threw herself around and ended up on the floor kicking and everyone stayed away and prayed it would end soon and that no one got hurt. When this happened, Bea's mom got so tense that she threw up and then started crying and had to retreat for a while. Even though she'd been dealing with it all of Aunt Claire's life, she still couldn't really function around it.

Bea thought she needed therapy. Her mom disagreed. The pattern continued on and on.

Dude get up. Sam texted Bea five times in a row, annoyed that Bea wasn't responding. The truth was, Bea was up, just in bed still, and had no interest in texting

Sam back. Sleeping super late was a good excuse for not responding to a friend you didn't like when it was still morning.

Plus, Bea wanted some more time with these fortune tellers from Ms. Steinhauer.

Bea pulled the small cardboard box off her night table and brought it into her bed. She sat up straight against all her throw pillows and flipped through the next fortune teller.

Face your fears

She flipped through again to see if she'd get the same fortune or a different one.

Tell people how you feel

And again.

It's never too late

She knew she was picking different things each time to get a different fortune, but she had to see all of them, and she didn't want to just peek to see the fortunes without really going through the process.

Right then Bea's laptop pinged from her desk, and she figured it was Sam texting her there instead—maybe using her email instead of her phone number.

But it wasn't Sam.

It was Nora.

Hi, Bea—I know we haven't talked in forever but text back if you get this. I hope you will. This iMessage is the only contact info I have for you so I hope it works. Not sure if you've gotten anything in the mail lately, too, but I've also been finding fortune tellers in strange places, when I know I threw them all out . . .

Bea stared at the text and read it over and over again. Just those few words from Nora made her smile, a sense of warmth surrounding her. It kind of felt like coming home after a long trip. Even though you're sad the trip is over, you're so happy to be back in your space with your things.

All Bea wanted was to be back with Nora and Millie somewhere, catch up on the past year and be friends again. Maybe they couldn't physically be back together at Shire, and they couldn't be in third or fourth grade again, making fortune tellers, but they could reconnect and start fresh.

She stared at her computer screen with her fingers resting on the keyboard, about to type back to Nora, when she heard someone pounding on her door.

"Bea!" the voice screamed. "WTH, girl."

It was Sam.

Somehow she'd shown up at her house, and maybe Bea's mom or Aunt Claire or maybe even Danny let her in. Bea's dad was at another professorial academic blah blah blah conference; he was MIA again. It seemed like he was always working.

"What is wrong with you?" Sam closed Bea's door and stood with her back against it. "You can't just keep ignoring me. Tell me honestly—do you want to be my friend or not? This is not cool, Bea. NOT COOL!" She yelled the last part.

"Oh my goodness, Sam. Calm down." Bea shook her head. "I just woke up. I got a text I had to respond to. My aunt had seizures all night. Seriously. Stop."

"It's always excuses with you," Sam said. "Honestly. Do you even realize that?"

"Sam." Bea swallowed hard and felt tears lumping up behind her eyes, dribbling out little by little. "Just stop, okay?"

"Oh my god, wait. You're crying?" Sam walked over to her then and put an arm over her shoulder, and all of a sudden seemed like the most sympathetic person in the world. *How is it possible that there are so many different versions of Sam?* Bea wondered.

"Sam, listen, it was just a long night." Bea paused. "Why don't you go downstairs and get a snack and then wait for me in the backyard, k? I'll get ready and then we'll go do something. Maybe roller skating in Brooklyn Bridge Park? We can take the bus."

Bea was doing all she could to seem enthusiastic and excited about a day with Sam. She was doing all she could to remain calm and not like she was about to freak out because of her unwavering need to write back to Nora.

"Okay, I guess I can do that." Sam breathed in and exhaled. "You're just kind of a mysterious person. Do you know that?"

Bea laughed and tried to act like this whole thing was funny and not a big deal when it was actually exactly the opposite. "I'll try and be less mysterious," she said.

Sam finally left Bea's room and Bea knew she only had a few minutes to write back to Nora, get dressed, brush her teeth, and be out in the backyard. She couldn't over-think this, but it was actually a huge moment and she wanted to make sure her response was just right.

Still, there was no time to debate it or think about it too much.

Hi, Nora—So good to hear from you. I got a box of fortune tellers in the mail and I HAVE BEEN FINDING THEM, TOO! We have to talk. Did Millie get anything? Do you know? Sorry so many questions. LOL.

Bea waited a minute to hit send but then she finally did and it felt like twenty cinder blocks were lifted off her shoulders. Right then, she actually got a feeling like she could sit up straighter and relax and breathe more deeply.

The funny thing was, after sending that text, Bea was sort of a little bit excited to spend the day with Sam. Being in communication with Nora, even the littlest bit, lifted Bea up, boosted her confidence and made Bea feel better about life in Kensington and life with Sam and starting seventh grade at Prenner.

Bea washed her face, brushed her teeth, threw on her favorite gray Aviator Nation tee and the most perfect pair of jean cutoffs ever created. She pulled her hair up into a tight bun, added her email to her iMessage on her phone so she'd get any responses from Nora there, and ran downstairs.

Danny was at the table with disheveled hair and a torn T-shirt, slurping a smoothie and watching something on YouTube on his phone.

"Your stalker's here again." Danny laughed.

Bea rolled her eyes even though he didn't even look up from his phone to notice. "I know. I saw her already. Who sent her up to my room?"

"No clue." He shrugged. "Mom took Aunt Claire shopping. She said not to spend all day inside."

"Noted." Bea cleared her throat, filled her water bottle, grabbed a protein bar, and went out to the backyard.

She found Sam in a bikini in the blow-up pool, chewing

furiously on the end of a straw from her iced coffee cup.

"This water is nasty, by the way," Sam said. "Do you guys ever empty this pool?"

Bea laughed. "Sam, you're pretty much the only one who uses it. Do you know that?"

"I do know that," Sam replied. "Still, though."

Bea waited a second to respond.

Okay, she pumped herself up. *I am determined to make today different with Sam, to start seventh grade with a good attitude.*

When Bea didn't say anything, Sam added, "I'm going to change and then let's go roller skating like you said. Sounds fun."

Bea waited for Sam outside and she tried super hard to not stare at her phone waiting for Nora to text back. But she couldn't help it. This little bit of contact with Nora filled her with a sense of completeness and happiness she hadn't felt since the party incident, since she'd left Shire and the Upper East Side.

Without Nora and Millie, she was incomplete. She knew that now. And she didn't want to spend any more time not talking to them.

"I decided I'm going to have a boyfriend this year," Sam declared when she got back outside to Bea's patio. "And I decided it's going to be one of Danny's friends." She paused. "And I decided you're going to make this happen for me."

Bea forced herself to take deep, calming breaths. This was just who Sam was, and it was okay. Bea would get used to it eventually. It was okay for them to be different from one another and still be friends and enjoy each other's company. The question was: Did she enjoy Sam's company at all?

She wasn't sure.

"So Danny's coming with us. And so are his friends," Sam went on with her list of declarations.

"Wait. What?" Bea realized she hadn't been paying attention.

"Yup. They're coming with us roller skating. I just talked to Danny inside." She pulled her hair into a high ponytail. "He loves me, by the way. But I'd never do that to you."

Bea laughed it off but didn't reply.

"What is going on? You're here, but not here like always. I thought it would be better when I got back from vacation, but it's not better."

"I'm fine. I'm here. All good about Danny and Danny's friends and whatever." Bea smiled. She wasn't going to let Sam get the best of her. Maybe that's what Sam wanted and it wasn't going to happen.

"Looks like I'm coming along after all," Danny said when he got outside. "Mom's gonna be pissed if we're not here when she gets home, though. She has a meeting tonight and wants someone to be here with Aunt Claire."

"She said that?" Bea asked, spraying some sunscreen on her arms.

"Yeah." Danny looked at Bea and Bea looked at Danny and then Bea wasn't sure if Danny was saying this so Bea could get out of this plan with Sam. Sometimes he looked out for his twin sister and sometimes he was as oblivious as most twelve-year-old boys are. It was hard to say what was happening in this moment, but Bea knew she didn't have much time to figure it out.

"So can you guys go or not?" Sam asked. "I can't deal with you and all of these wishy-washy plans."

"Sam, calm down," Bea said. "This is just how it is with our aunt living with us."

Knowing she couldn't really criticize that any more than she already had, Sam stayed quiet.

At that exact second, Bea's phone chimed—she'd switched it to volume-on since she was waiting for Nora's reply with too high of an intensity for the vibrate setting.

"Whoa, way to have your phone on high alert. Are you the president now or something?" Sam asked. Danny looked alarmed, too, since Bea's phone was never volume-on since for the most part she wanted to avoid all communication.

"We're good to go," Bea said, reading her phone. "But give me just one minute."

She ran inside before either of them had a chance to moan or groan or say they were leaving without her. They wouldn't do that, anyway. Bea knew that.

Bea leaned on the kitchen island and read the text three times.

It was from Nora.

Putting the three of us on this thread together.
Okay.
So
1. I got fortune tellers in the mail from Ms. Steinhauer
. . . (Millie, she didn't have your address but I have some for you.)
2. Bea, did you get any in the mail?
3. Did you guys see that email about the future of Shire day?
4. I miss you both so much.
5. Can we please be friends again?
6. Quinn Afisch doesn't matter. I'm sorry I thought she did. I'm also sorry I was mean to you about the fortune tellers, Millie.
7. Love and party canoe.

Bea burst into tears. *Love and party canoe* was their catchphrase they'd come up with after they went through every single Shire yearbook for the last twenty-five years one day at recess and discovered that the graduating class of 2002—way before they were even born—was *Party Canoe Class of 2002*. The three of them

thought it was so funny that they made it their catchphrase, too.

It was one of those things that was only funny to them
but it didn't matter because it was SO funny to them. The
most funny, actually.

That was sort of what friendship was all about. Very
specific, simple, random things that were so funny to
small group of besties.

Bea waited a second to respond to see if Millie would
write first, but when she didn't, Bea said:

1. Yes I got them & I have no idea what is happening
but I need to find out.
2. Got the email and want to go, since I live the
closest.
3. I miss you both, too. SO MUCH.
4. Yes, let's please be friends forever and never stop
being friends again.
5. Quinn Afisch who? LOL
6. Love and party canoe.

"Bea! Come on!" Sam screamed at Bea from outside.
"Danny and I are leaving in two minutes whether you're
out here or not. I'm gonna force him to make out with
me. . . ."

"Ew! What!" Bea heard Danny chirp back and then Bea
laughed to herself, still leaning over the kitchen island,

giving Millie one more second to chime in on the group text.

Just the idea that there was a group text between the three of them filled Bea with an off-the-charts kind of happiness she had forgotten was even possible.

So what if Sam was pretty awful and only cared about herself? So what if her mom was preoccupied with Aunt Clare and they lived way out in Brooklyn and she had to start school tomorrow?

All of that would be okay because she had Millie and Nora back.

At least she thought she had them back.

No matter what—they were at least talking.

That felt like the first step on the path to everything being awesome again.

CHAPTER 18

Nora

NORA WAS SO PROUD OF herself for being the first one to initiate a group text that she almost wanted to throw herself a little party. Of course she wasn't going to because that would be weird, but that was how she felt.

But since she had blamed herself for the whole thing all this time, she had to be the one to get them all talking again.

Her phone chimed with a text from Millie. Finally.

1. I haven't gotten anything in the mail! But the fortune tellers have appeared in my life again . . . spooky.

2. Got the email but don't think we can go. ☹

3. The amount of missing I have for the two of you is literally off the charts and cannot even be measured.

4. Let's make a pact to never fight or stop talking ever again, no matter what.

5. Not even going to type out QA's full name. And I forgive you. (I think.)

6. Love and party canoe!!!!!!!!!!!! XOXOXO

Millie's text was so Millie it was hard to believe. She was always taking things up a notch and that's what Nora loved about her. Well, one of the things. Nora loved a lot about Millie. Mostly everything. Except the fact that she always felt left out. But so what? Everyone felt left out sometimes.

FaceTime tonight at 8 p.m., okay? Nora wrote, and waited for a response. But no one wrote back right away, and then she started to get nervous all over again. Maybe it was too soon for FaceTime. Maybe they needed to text more first before seeing each other's faces.

While she waited, Nora took a few fortune tellers out of the box from Ms. Steinhauer.

As Nora put her fingers in the slots, she had this unwavering feeling that whatever this particular fortune said was going to guide her entire seventh-grade year. She couldn't explain why—it was a feeling she had, and her feelings were rarely wrong.

P-I-N-K

S-I-X

H-E-A-R-T

Wherever you're going: show up on time

This wasn't really a fortune; it was way more of an instruction. Unfair.

"Nor, time to go!" her mom yelled from downstairs. "Dad's going to be mad if we're late."

That wasn't true, but her mom always tried to paint her dad as the bad guy. He *was* the bad guy, in Nora's mind, because he was the one who wanted the divorce. But caring if they were late? He wouldn't. *He* was always late.

She looked at the fortune teller again.

Wherever you're going: show up on time

Her whole body felt shivery.

"Can we just stay for deli dinner and then come home?" Penelope whined.

"It'll be fine," their mom said. "You'll come home first thing tomorrow. We'll get everything set for school the next day. While you're at Dad's, I'll clear out all the old supplies from last year. How does that sound?"

Nora laughed a little to herself. It was like her mom

expected Penelope to get all excited about getting rid of old supplies.

By the time Nora made it downstairs, her mom and sister were already in the mudroom with their shoes on, and they seemed annoyed that she was taking so long.

"I just don't understand why we have to sleep at Dad's," Penelope said in the car. "He doesn't even care if our rooms are nice, and he doesn't have a real table, we eat on stack tables—did you even know that? It doesn't feel like home."

"It's fine, Pen," Nora groaned, while at the same time remembering that she was supposed to go out with Esme and Jade tonight. They had planned to get some final back-to-school clothes at the Miracle Mile and then get dinner at Shake it Up, Tressdale's burger and fries and shakes place. Their Oreo shake was one of the best parts of Tressdale, Nora thought.

"It's fine for you because you won't even be there!" Penelope yelled. Clearly she'd remembered Nora's plans even though Nora hadn't.

"What do you mean she won't be there?" Nora's mom asked, her antennae up in a way Nora really didn't like.

"She always goes out with her friends when we stay at Dad's," Penelope explained, and Nora sank lower into the front seat, like she could somehow disappear and her mom would stop asking questions about this. "Like every time, and then it's just Dad and me for dinner, and he orders a pizza but not even from Nick's and it's so greasy and bad and then we just sit there and he puts on cartoons and I don't even like cartoons!"

Penelope screamed the last part and then burst into tears, and Nora's mom had to pull over to comfort her. Their mom got out of the car on the side of the road (it wasn't a busy street, but still) and climbed in the back seat with Penelope and let her cry on her shoulder.

Oh lord, here we go, Nora thought. *How long are we going to be dealing with this?*

FaceTime at 8 works for me, Bea responded, and then Millie said *Same!* And then Nora realized she had a problem on her hands. She'd double-booked the night—triple-booked if she counted the fact that she was really supposed to be hanging with her dad and Penelope.

But she couldn't bail on Bea and Millie now. No way. That was most important.

Great, call you then, Party (Canoe) People!

"Oh my goodness!" her mom yelled. "These chimes are driving me nuts. Your sister is clearly upset and you're just sitting there texting! Please! Have some sensitivity."

Nora was grateful she was still in the front seat, looking ahead so her mom couldn't see the deepest eye roll Nora had ever done. She was about to tell her she had finally reconnected with Millie and Bea—which would probably make her mom the happiest person in the world—but she didn't. The focus was on Penelope right now and maybe that was actually going to benefit Nora, too.

Maybe they'd get out of another night in their dad's depressing beige apartment.

It wasn't like Nora disagreed with her sister. Going there was pretty much the least fun. It was hard for Nora to even remember if they used to have fun with their dad back in Manhattan. They probably did, but doing what? He was always kind of absent and distracted, missing band concerts and coming late to parent-teacher conferences.

Why did they have to go spend the night at his place?

Penelope was right. Dinner and coming home seemed like a way better plan. The only good part was that he'd said they were having dinner from the deli tonight, and at least she'd remembered to remind him to ask for extra half-sour pickles. *So the food will be good and maybe dinner part won't be torture*, Nora thought.

At least. At least. At least. This was always how she got through the less-than-fun things.

"I agree with Penelope," Nora said finally. "I don't want to stay there, either. Can you guys, like, adjust your divorce agreement or whatever? Shouldn't we get a say?"

"Nora June," her mom said in a tone that sounded like she was doing whatever she could to stay calm. "I don't like how you're speaking to me. I don't like it one bit."

Nora decided to stay silent the rest of the ride. She had way too much on her mind to worry about dealing with her mother right now.

CHAPTER 19

Flashback—December of fourth grade

NORA, BEA, AND MILLIE WERE on the speckled gray carpet in Ms. Giroux's room during one of their morning "five-minute chats with Ms. Giroux."

"This is the best way to start the day," Millie declared.

"It is, isn't it?" Ms. Giroux asked. "And to think it only took me twenty years to think of it. . . . So, my girls. What's on your mind?"

Bea was in the middle of making a fortune teller.

"Bea? Are you with us?" Ms. Giroux asked.

"Sorry, yes. Wanted to finish ten before ten a.m.!"

Everyone giggled.

"Oh, Bea. I love how you're always challenging yourself." Ms. Giroux smiled.

"So, here's what's on my mind." Millie launched into what everyone thought was going to be a long speech.

"We love making these fortune tellers! Can we sell them and donate the money for a pizza party or something?"

"Oh! A lovely idea!" Ms. Giroux clapped. "I'll mention it to Mr. Hidgur."

Once they got the go-ahead from Mr. Hidgur, the head of school, the girls spent the next three days making over three hundred fortune tellers, and on the Tuesday after Martin Luther King, Jr., Day, they launched the first-ever Fortune Teller Fundraiser.

"Fifty cents a fortune teller," Nora yelled from the table in the lobby.

"Fifty cents to know your destiny," Bea echoed.

Darren McCreer stood in front of them, going through the motions. "My destiny is to eat pickles every day for lunch?!" he yelped.

"Do you like pickles?" Felix Yades asked.

"I love pickles!" Darren exclaimed. "This is a dream come true!"

Millie, Bea, and Nora exchanged high fives and went back to promoting the fortune tellers. Eventually, they sold out of all of them.

By the end of the day, they had $150 for pizza for their entire grade.

"Mission accomplished," Millie said as they packed up at their lockers.

"Mission more than accomplished," Nora added. "We get to see Darren eat pickles every day for lunch!"

They all cracked up and walked home together, arms linked, smiles so wide their cheeks hurt.

"Think we can make another three hundred at our sleepover Friday?" Millie asked.

"Oh yes," Bea replied. "We definitely can."

CHAPTER 20

Millie

THE GIRLS' FACETIME GOT POSTPONED because Nora's dad declared it a screen-free night, but Millie wasn't totally upset about that. She was still trying to navigate the Rodge situation and prepare for the first day of school.

There was A LOT going on.

The good news was that Nora was mailing some of the fortune tellers to Millie. The other good news was that Millie, Nora, and Bea all pretty much had the same first day of school. Bea's was just an orientation, but still. Millie's cousin Astrid in Arizona had literally started school in the middle of August. It always shocked Millie. The middle of summer and Astrid was in a scratchy uniform skirt on an uncomfortable chair in a classroom. It just wasn't right.

But even though the FaceTime call was postponed, the group text was on in full force, way more than it had ever been before.

Millie: Good luck today friends
Nora: Ack, same to you both
Nora: Wish we were together
Bea: Ugh me too, times a million
Bea: So glad it's only orientation though. NOT READY but wish it wasn't on the same day as the event at Shire ☹
Millie: Praying the box you sent comes today, Nora.

No one responded after that and Millie figured they were on their way to school. She was texting on the way to the bus stop at the edge of Sheffield Shores.

Rodge was already there when she arrived, and her stomach fluttered. Millie wasn't sure how to approach him or what to say. They hadn't spoken at all since the food pantry discussion and every thought that popped into Millie's head seemed wrong, so she froze just as she was about to let the words come out of her mouth.

She'd texted him a few times to check in and he hadn't responded, but somehow it hadn't occurred to her that they'd be alone at the bus stop together.

He was just sitting there, on the edge of the curb, looking to the left to see if the bus was coming, and since it was just the two of them, Millie knew she had to say something.

"How are you feeling about the first day?" she asked.

"Eh." He shrugged.

She waited for him to say more, but he didn't, and that only made her stomach flutter even more. A part of her wished she'd never talked to him in the first place, wished they'd never gone to Bear's Den together for chicken fingers or even down to the lake. Millie almost wished he was just some stranger at the bus stop, some new kid, and she could introduce herself and they could start fresh.

But none of that was possible.

"Listen, Rodge." She sat down next to him and then realized they were way too close to one another, so she scooched away just the tiniest bit. Millie was worried she had poppy seeds in her teeth and bad breath—she regretted the bagel with scallion cream cheese she'd eaten on the walk over. "I'm sorry I didn't know what to say about the food pantry. There's nothing at all to be embarrassed about."

He didn't answer her immediately.

A moment later he said, "That's easy for you to say, because you're not in my situation. But I appreciate you mentioning it."

Millie sighed. She knew what to say now. It came to her like a miracle somehow. "Here's the thing. Maybe I don't know specifically this exact situation. But I think I know a little bit about how you're feeling."

Rodge looked at her, like he was suspicious about what she was saying. "You do?"

"I do. Want to know how?"

He nodded.

It almost seemed like they were playing some kind of game, even though that wasn't Millie's intention at all.

"So my dad was a super when we lived in the city, kind of like how he's the super at Sheffield Shores, like he manages everything and fixes stuff, you know what I mean?"

Rodge nodded again.

"So all of my friends had parents with fancier jobs and nicer apartments and ours was so small and I always felt like the poorest kid at school. Sabrina and I were on a full scholarship and stuff," Millie explained. "So I get it. I know what it's like to feel different. Really, really different."

Rodge was silent.

Finally, he asked, "So how did that work out for you? I mean, like, with friends and stuff?"

Millie shrugged. "I dunno. I mean, like, we just sort of didn't talk about it that much. Here I'm different because there's, like, no one Jewish besides us, and I live in this really rural area now when I'm used to the city, so that's like a whole other adjustment."

"And how's that going?"

"Not well." Millie laughed. "I haven't made a single friend!"

"You told me everyone was nice!" Rodge yelled.

"Well, yeah, I wanted to make you feel comfortable. It was a white lie, I guess." Millie hid her face behind her hands. "I'm sorry! We'll meet friends together!"

"Whatever you say." Rodge laughed. "Life, man, am I right?"

"I think you're supposed to run those words together," Millie explained. "Like amIright?"

After that, they both fully cracked up and Millie couldn't even really remember how the conversation started and evolved and how they'd ended up here. But she was sure Rodge felt a little more comfortable now, so that was a good thing.

Right then, Millie's phone buzzed, and Rodge said, "See, you do have friends, someone's texting you!"

"Could be my mom." Millie laughed.

"Touché."

But it wasn't her mom. It was the group text again.

Bea: Guys this keeps getting weirder and weirder

Bea: did anyone else get a fortune before school?

Nora: What do you mean by get a fortune?

Bea: hahahaha like use the fortune teller?

Nora: of course . . .

Millie: I did too . . .

Bea: anyone remember writing inspirational quotes?

Millie gasped.

"What?" Rodge asked.

She responded to the group before answering him.

Millie: the best mirror is an old friend?

Bea: SAME. FREAKY

Millie: ME TOO. SO FREAKY

Nora: What is going on for real

Millie smiled so wide and so long her cheeks started to hurt. The three of them hadn't even heard each other's voices or seen each other's faces, but they were connected again. On a cosmic, getting-the-same-fortunes level. No doubt about it. And that made Millie feel maybe even happy for the first time in forever and ever.

Nora: Okay FaceTime tonight for real, okay? So we can discuss first days and stuff. I have soooo much to tell you.

Millie: Same. It's on.

Bea: 8 p.m.

Bea: FOR REAL THIS TIME

"Who are you texting like the world is suddenly on fire?" Rodge asked her. "Seems like something really important is going on. . . ."

"Well, you know how you said you like mysteries?" Millie asked him, lifting her eyebrows.

"I do. I remember saying that, and it is in fact the truth."

"So sit back, relax, and get ready for this one. . . ." She looked at him. "Well, I guess you can't sit back since we're on a curb and I see the bus coming, anyway, so there's not that much time, but . . ."

"Just say it, Millie. Sheesh."

"The fortune tellers keep showing up. It wasn't just at Bear's Den that day. And it's not only happening to me. It's happening to my friends, too. My friends from Shire who I haven't talked to since fifth grade. All of a sudden. To all of us. And we all got the same fortune today." She paused. "Care to solve that one?"

His eyes bulged. "Wow. I'm going to need some more information."

The bus came then, and soon Rodge and Millie were on their way to their first day of seventh grade at Sheffield Middle. Millie was still nervous.

But maybe, just maybe, things were going to be better than they ever were before.

CHAPTER 21

Bea

SO FAR, ORIENTATION WASN'T AS bad as Bea had expected. It was basically just sitting in the auditorium listening to a zillion speeches with a break for breakfast and then a break for lunch. Prenner always fed them very well. That was one good thing about the place.

Bea wanted to just sit there and zone out, stare out the window, and imagine Nora and Millie on their first days of seventh grade.

It had become a routine for her. Every day in sixth grade, she'd sit there in her classes and picture what Nora and Millie were doing, what they were learning, who they were sitting with at lunch. She'd dream of the three of them together, still at Shire, coming up with alternate scenarios where they were all back in their old life, where the Quinn Afisch incident never happened, where

Bea was still sleeping in her tiny room in Manhattan, one of those stuffed animal hammocks in the corner.

Bea and Sam were among the first ones in the cafeteria for their midmorning breakfast when a girl pulled out a chair, about to sit down next to Bea. "Oh, I think you dropped this," she said, picking something up off the floor.

Bea knew her face was bright red. She imagined she looked as embarrassed as she felt.

That was one thing about herself she really wanted to change: her inability to not show embarrassment. Somehow it was impossible for her.

"OMG!" Sam scoffed, looking at what Bea held in her hands. "Blast from the past! I loved those things! That's yours, Bea?"

"Um, I seriously have no clue where it came from."

"Is it yours?" Sam asked.

Bea planned to lie. Of course she did. She couldn't tell Sam and this entire table that she'd brought a fortune teller that she (or Millie or Nora) had made years ago to her first day of seventh grade, to ease her nerves and guide her.

"Um, no." Bea shook her head. "I have no idea what this is."

But her face was a cherry tomato and her cheeks were a billion degrees and Bea was the worst liar in the world. If they believed her, it would be a miracle.

"I used to love these things so much," Sam said. "Give it to me."

Bea hesitated, though. She didn't want to give it to her. What if she didn't get it back? What if this specific fortune teller was going to tell her something she needed to know?

"I'll just throw it away," Bea stammered.

"Why? You're being so weird. Yet again." Sam rolled her eyes, sort of in the direction of the others at the table, but since she didn't know any of them, it fell pretty flat.

"Well, it's not yours, and it could be, like, private or something." Just then Bea had a solution. It landed on her brain like a perfect ladybug. "It's probably one of the third graders' or something. I should go turn it in. I bet someone's looking for it."

She stood up before anyone had a chance to reply, and soon she was leaving the Prenner cafeteria and heading down the hallway.

She sat down on the bench outside the main office, and took some deep breaths, and tried to ignore her stomach gurgling and rumbling. It was telling her to get back to breakfast.

As she took deep breaths, she went through the fortune teller.

O-R-A-N-G-E

D-R-A-G-O-N (Millie's dragon drawing was seriously

on point. She was the only one of the three of them who could draw.)

F-O-U-R

Go back to where you started

They weren't really allowed to have phones in school, but at that moment, she didn't care. She pulled her phone out of her backpack and snapped a picture of the fortune to send to Nora and Millie.

As she was sending the text message with the photo, an Instagram notification popped up. The Shire School had posted.

It was a picture of the school building with the caption REMINDER: TODAY! *Day to discuss Shire's future. See you there!*

There was no doubt about it. She had to be there. The fortune. This notification. All of it.

She had to go.

If she left right now, she'd make it to the Upper East Side by eleven.

Bea shoved the fortune teller in her pocket and ran to the nurse's office.

"Um, I'm really sick, my stomach is all messed up," Bea told Ms. Sraich, Prenner's nurse.

"Oh, I'm sorry to hear, doll." She scrunched up her

nose. "Sure it's not just nerves? Orientation and all . . ."

"Oh, I'm sure." Bea picked at the cuticle on her right thumb.

Ms. Sraich looked up Bea's account and saw that her file said she could self-dismiss. "You're okay to go home on your own?"

Bea nodded. "Definitely."

"I still need to reach a parent before I let you go, though," she said.

Finally, on the third try, she reached Bea's mom, who was on her way to see that doctor in Boston with Aunt Claire again.

"I have Bea in my office, Mrs. Grellick," the nurse said. "I know she has self-dismiss privileges but wanted to let you know before she heads home." Pause. "She says it's her stomach." Pause. "Okay, I'll tell her. Okay. Right. Take care."

Ms. Sraich hung up the phone. "Okay, your mom says to head home and she'll be in touch with you, and the heating pad is in the cabinet under the TV in the den."

"Thank you. Rough way to start the school year." Bea shook her head, trying to sell it. "Hopefully it passes quickly."

She didn't have a chance to say goodbye to Sam, or anyone. She ran out of Prenner and sprinted to the 6 train.

Bea faked sick, left school, and took the subway all the

way from Brooklyn to the Upper East Side, and she didn't tell her parents she was going there.

All of this was wrong; she knew that. But all of it was necessary.

When Bea got off the train and looked around, she realized she hadn't been in her old neighborhood in a really long time. Actually, she couldn't even remember when she'd been here last. That realization turned her stomach sour.

On her way to Shire, Bea passed the playground where she and her friends had spent many afternoons playing ice cream shop, going up the slide instead of down, and climbing to the top of the monkey bars so they could sit on them. She passed their favorite bagel place and their favorite pizza shop, and her old apartment building.

She reached into her pocket for the fortune teller the girl had found on the floor before. Bea needed another fortune.

B-L-U-E

T-W-O

B-I-R-D

Don't doubt yourself. You have all the tools you need.

Bea stared at it; her phone buzzed in her pocket.

It was Danny. An actual phone call.

"Hello?" Bea answered.

"Are you okay? I was looking for you, and the nurse said you went home sick."

Bea didn't answer.

"Bea? Hello?" Danny asked.

"Oh, um, yeah. I'm fine." She paused. "So sorry. I'll explain later."

"Bea, don't be dumb. I can see your location and I can see that you're standing right outside of Shire."

Right. Tracking.

Her whole family tracked each other.

Hopefully her mom would be too preoccupied with Aunt Claire and the Boston doctor to track her.

"Danny, stop. I'm fine. I just need to take care of something, okay?" Bea hung up before Danny had a chance to answer. There was no way to explain all of this now, so it wasn't even worth trying or starting. He'd probably never understand it anyway.

Bea ran up the steps to Shire's front door before she convinced herself not to. Within minutes, she was hitting the buzzer, her heart pounding, tears streaming down her face. She wiped them away with the sleeve of her jean jacket and took three deep breaths.

Not a good idea to go inside crying, Bea told herself.

As soon as Bea was buzzed in, she stopped at the main desk to say hi to Mr. Lou, the security guy.

"Am I seeing who I think I'm seeing?" Mr. Lou asked. "Is that Bea Grellick?"

"Hi, Mr. Lou," Bea said softly. "How are you?"

Hold back the tears, she told herself. *Hold back the tears.*

"Hanging in, hanging in." Mr. Lou smiled his soft smile. It reminded Bea of towels just coming out of the dryer. "Not the same without all of you, of course. We're much smaller these days; the halls aren't as lively . . ."

Bea nodded. "I'm sure. I miss everyone so much."

"Oh boy, do we miss you, and Danny, of course," Mr. Lou answered. "Oh, I'm talking too much! Everyone's in the auditorium, go on!"

"Thanks." Bea smiled.

She couldn't bring herself to go in, though. She didn't want to see anyone. Bea wanted to be invisible but hear everything. So she did the next best thing. She stood in the back and listened, and luckily she arrived right when everyone was seated, facing the front.

"First of all, thank you all for coming today," Mr. Hidgur started. "I'm sorry about all the rumors that circulated about us not opening this fall. It's true that we are renting the lower school classrooms out, but not during the school day, so please do not worry about issues of safety and people in the building. While we don't know what the future brings after this school year, we want to bring our ALL to the present day. Help us fundraise! Help us

CELEBRATE SHIRE! We want all of you to be the voice of Shire, share our strengths with others, invite people to take tours, be our PR leaders, be our ambassadors!"

It all made sense right then. Everything clicked into place.

Why the fortune tellers appeared out of nowhere.

Of course their main mission was bringing the friends back together.

But there was more! What she needed to do. What *they* could do!

Celebrate Shire. An actual event. Bringing everyone back together—not for a gloomy day where everyone felt depressed, but a chance to really celebrate what made Shire special.

Bea looked all over the auditorium, and soon realized the person she wanted to see most wasn't in there.

She walked back to Mr. Lou at the front desk. He would know.

"Is Ms. Steinhauer here?" Bea asked, nervous but forcing herself to sound confident. Well, at least trying to sound confident.

"I believe she is—still working on cleaning out that classroom." He shook his head. "Oh boy, what a task! Thirty years she spent in there. . . . Remember where it is?"

Bea laughed. "Of course I do."

Bea choked back her tears yet again and trudged

the three flights up to Ms. Steinhauer's classroom. She peeked in before Ms. Steinhauer saw her. The bulletin boards were bare; boxes were stacked up nearly to the ceiling. Bookshelves were empty, and Ms. Steinhauer was sitting on her small silver stool—her gray spiral curls in a million different directions—staring out the window.

Bea wasn't sure how long she'd need to stand there before Ms. Steinhauer saw her, and she knew she had to get home eventually so she better just say hi and stop spying. Bea couldn't bring herself to hear any more about Shire's future. Mr. Hidgur was putting on a brave face, but there was sadness and fear underneath it.

"Ms. Steinhauer?" Bea said softly.

"Oh my goodness!" She stood up. "Is that my Bea?"

Bea didn't even respond. She just walked straight into the familiar classroom and put her arms around Ms. Steinhauer, and they hugged like relatives who had been apart for years and years. It seemed like they could've stayed in that hug for hours, and neither of them would have minded.

Bea wondered if most people hugged their old teachers this way, and she figured they probably didn't. That was another reason why Shire was so special.

"You came to Future of Shire Day?" Ms. Steinhauer asked, finally pulling away from the hug. "I think that's what they're calling it!"

"Well, kind of. Mostly, I came to talk to you!"

"You did? You got my package?"

Bea nodded. "Yes. And it's way spookier than you'll ever believe."

"Spooky?" Ms. Steinhauer's eyebrows crinkled together. "Come sit."

So Bea sat down and she explained the whole thing, how she, Millie, and Nora had been finding the fortune tellers before the boxes from Ms. Steinhauer arrived. And how the fortunes eerily corresponded to what the girls were going through, even though they never wrote fortunes like that. And how the fortunes had brought the girls back together. How they were talking again and maybe even on the path to being friends again.

"Back in the day, we wrote silly, nonsense, little-kid fortunes and now they have, like, meanings to them," Bea told her. "It's soo sooo eerie!"

"Wow, really?"

"Yes. But the thing is, and I didn't realize this until I came here today, but I think these fortune tellers can save the school."

"Oh, Bea . . ." Ms. Steinhauer looked off into the distance. "I'm not sure what's possible at this point. As you know, the lower school is gone, and the middle school maybe only has one year left. And then—"

"There's still hope!" Bea said, sniffling. "Really. This place is magical. We made magical fortune tellers here.

We can save it. We can tell everyone how special it is. Seriously!"

Ms. Steinhauer sat down in her armchair—the one that had been in her classroom for decades, where she'd probably read thousands of books aloud to her students. "Magical fortune tellers, hmm," she said. "How does that happen? What makes them magical?"

Bea wanted to bring up the whole *Write Your Destiny* thing from the markers, but she also didn't really think she had time for this kind of conversation. She had faked sick, left orientation, and she definitely wasn't supposed to be here, and what difference did it make where the magic came from? She had an event to plan, a school to save, the most perfect friendship in the world to get back on track.

"There's a lot to discuss." Bea bit her lip. "I need to get back to Brooklyn, but will you help me plan this? It'll basically just be, like, a celebration of the school, kind of—and we'll invite alumni and whoever is around, and I don't know, we'll see. Maybe we can make it a fundraiser? Maybe someone from the *New York Times* can come? Maybe we'll sell the fortune tellers. Mr. Hidgur was just saying he wanted ideas, wanted people to be Shire ambassadors, so . . ."

Ms. Steinhauer smiled and wiped away a tear trickling out of the corner of her eye. "Oh, Bea. You're one of the brightest lights I've ever encountered. Do you know that?"

Bea honestly didn't know it. In fact, lately Bea felt dull and boring, like oatmeal that had been sitting in the pot too long.

"Let me talk to Mr. Hidgur, okay?" Ms. Steinhauer said softly. "I hope we can make this happen. Your tenacity is contagious." She paused. "I want to make this happen."

After that, they both stood up and hugged, and Bea left Shire and sprinted all the way to the subway. Her heart pounded from running so fast and from her excitement, but also her fear that she was going to get in major trouble.

The train came right away and luckily enough, she got a seat.

Grateful for Wi-Fi on the subway, she typed out a text quicker than she'd typed anything in her whole life.

Bea: I faked sick and left orientation and went to the Future of Shire day or whatever it's called. I saw Ms. Steinhauer. So much to tell you.
Millie: YES YES YES ALL THE YESSSSSSES IN THE WORLD
Nora: I WANT TO HEAR ALL

CHAPTER 22

Nora

"I HAVE A VERY IMPORTANT call at eight," Nora announced to Penelope and her mom that night. They had a tradition where they always ate sushi for dinner on the first day of school. They each had one piece left and they were about to do a "sushi-cheers" to start the year off on the right note.

"Ooooh, Jeremy?" Penelope squeaked. Somehow she seemed to know everything going on in her older sister's life, even though Nora never told her anything.

"No. Not Jeremy." Nora paused. "But let's just do our clink-not-clink so I can go get ready, k?"

They called it a clink-not-clink, like how you'd cheers with wine glasses, but since sushi didn't make a sound, could it really be a clink?

"I want you both to have an amazing year," their mom

said, sniffling. She was always on the verge of tears. "I'm so proud of you. I love you so much. You're my treasures, my greatest gifts . . ."

"Okay, Mom," Penelope interrupted. "We get it. Cool. Thanks."

"I love you both," Nora said, and got up from the table, and then laughed to herself a little bit because it sounded like she was leaving for some intense journey when really she was just going upstairs for a FaceTime.

"Thanks for not helping to clean up," Penelope grumbled.

"I told you I had a call!"

"Girls, calm down," their mom said, exasperated. "I'll take care of it tonight."

Upstairs in her room, Nora sat back against all her pillows and opened her laptop so she could prop her cell phone on it while she was on FaceTime. Plus this would be helpful if they had to do any research while they were chatting.

At eight p.m. on the dot, Nora started the call. She clicked on the group text, and then the video icon, and thirty seconds later, there they were.

Bea with her hair in pigtails, just out of the shower. This was her nighttime routine. She said it added a certain level of bounciness to her waves—she'd been doing it forever. And Millie, her wide smile, her dimples, her reddish-brown hair in a messy bun, like always.

"Oh my goodness, I can't even believe this is happening right now," Nora said. "Your faces on my screen. Literally cannot."

"Also cannot," Bea replied.

"Same level of cannot," Millie added, giggling.

"Can we please discuss that something seriously super freaky is going on with these fortune tellers?" Nora asked. She almost felt like she was running a meeting and following an actual agenda.

Sounding a little rigid, Nora. Gotta be more go-with-the-flow here.

"So super freaky," Millie answered. "Like, they're just sort of appearing. One showed up at the counter of our little diner type place when I was out with this guy and OMG."

"You were out with a guy?!" Nora and Bea shrieked at the same time, and then they all burst out laughing.

This is the best feeling in the world, Nora realized. Just to be able to laugh with people who understood you, who knew you. Even if all that time had passed, not so much had changed. She was sure they still understood her.

"Well, putting the out-with-a-guy thing aside for now," Millie continued, "what happened at Shire today?"

Bea sighed. "It's not great. I mean, there's no lower school, and middle and upper are small, but there's still hope, according to what I heard today." She paused. "And they want fundraising ideas; they want people to be ambassadors and stuff. So, like, what if we did a fundraiser? Like old-school. With the fortune tellers?"

"Um." Millie sat back in the armchair she was in. She looked like an actress in an old movie or someone about to give a lecture. It didn't even seem like something her mother would buy, Nora decided. Maybe wherever she was living now had come furnished. Nora's mind was going in a million different directions, and she had to get her thoughts back on track. "I mean, I don't think that could be enough, but maybe . . ."

Nora listened, trying to take it all in. She couldn't say anything for some reason. Not yet, anyway.

"What I mean is, yes it's a fundraiser, but it's also a celebration of Shire!" Bea exclaimed. "Like a last-ditch effort to show the magic of the place, and we come back, and we have our fortune tellers, and Ms. Steinhauer makes a speech. Maybe we try to find all the famous alumni to come back. And we close the street, and we all celebrate and have Shire Sundaes. I don't know. All the things!"

"But will that help?" Nora asked finally. "Not to be a downer, but is it too late? I mean, we all moved away. The pandemic happened. The school practically evaporated; the lower school did evaporate." She felt sad all over again, like yeah, talking together was fun, but they'd never be back together again.

Millie sighed. "Well, like, it wouldn't hurt, right? Because even if Shire closes, at least there'd be one last hurrah—a chance to celebrate all it was."

"Yes! Exactly!" Bea smiled. "Ms. Steinhauer said she'd talk to Mr. Hidgur and let me know. But based on what he was saying today, it seems like it can maybe work?"

They all sat there silently for a moment, and Nora wondered how this call had gone in so many different directions and if it was all impossible.

At that exact second, she was getting an incoming group FaceTime from Jade and Esme.

Ignore. Decline. No time for that now.

Jade: Ignoring us, Nor-Nor?

Esme: hellloooo

Nora: so so sorry, in the middle of something, can't talk rn

Nora, Bea, and Millie stayed on FaceTime for another hour going around and around about all of this, not settling on any decision one way or another. It seemed like there were so many options for them to try and also no options all at the same time.

But there was good news: the three of them were talking again—*almost* in person—and that turned Nora's heart a shade of neon pink.

CHAPTER 23

Millie

MILLIE'S BOX OF FORTUNE TELLERS from Nora arrived and she was so excited to dive into them.

She was done getting dressed, and about to have breakfast, when she pulled the next fortune teller out of the box. It was a little smooshed but she was able to get it back into shape pretty quickly.

R-E-D

F-I-V-E

M-O-N-K-E-Y

Don't give up on your goals, even when things are hard

She picked up her phone to text Bea and Nora and then at that exact second, it vibrated. Texts from both of them. Pictures actually.

Don't give up on your goals, even when things are
hard

OMG

OMG

OMG

They had all gotten the same exact fortune! On the
same exact day again!

Millie only had a few minutes to grab breakfast and
head to the bus, but she started a group FaceTime anyway.

"Guys," she said as soon as they answered. "This is so
spooky."

"It really is," Nora said. "I'm so late and I'm going to
miss the bus and I need to hang up this call so I can run
but seriously. We need to make this Shire event happen.
I need to see you guys! Like now."

"Agree," Bea said. "Praying I hear back from Ms. Steinhauer soon."

"Same," Millie replied. "Love and party canoe!"

They all giggled.

"Love and party canoe forever," Nora said, and then
they hung up.

Millie ran to the pantry to get a protein bar and then
she sprinted to the bus stop without even saying goodbye to her parents.

Rodge was already there, sitting on the edge of the

curb, looking down at his sneakers. Millie noticed they were torn and she felt bad, figuring he'd probably wanted new sneakers for the start of the school year.

He looked so cute, though, his dirty-blond hair all messy and shaggy and then when he heard Millie coming, he looked up and smiled, and she realized he actually had really long eyelashes. Maybe she loved Rodge, she decided, and maybe she needed to make more of an effort with him. She'd have to ask Nora and Bea what to do, eventually. They would know.

"So get this." Millie sat down next to him.

"Yeah?"

"My friends and I all got the same exact fortune today," Millie explained. "Again!"

"Really?"

She nodded. "Yeah, we all have a box of these old fortune tellers we made a long time ago, so we've been going through them. And today, we all get the same exact fortune! Also, this has happened before."

"What!" Rodge yelled. "That's ridiculous." He paused. "But wait, how many did you make of the same one? Maybe it's actually not that crazy."

"I don't remember." Millie shook her head. "We made most of them in third and fourth grades."

Rodge laughed. "So what was the fortune?"

"Promise not to think it's cringe?" Millie asked.

"I can't promise that. I laugh a lot," Rodge said. "But I'll try my best."

"Fine. That's fair." Millie shrugged.

"So what was it?" Rodge asked again.

"Oh yeah. Okay." Millie paused, her stomach feeling fluttery all of a sudden. "Don't give up on your goals, even when things are hard."

"Pretty inspirational for a third grader," Rodge said. "I'm impressed."

Millie smiled. "Right?"

She couldn't tell him the really eerie part—that they'd never have written this; that they only wrote silly, ridiculous fortunes. He'd never believe her.

"But are things ever that hard for third graders?" Rodge asked just as the bus pulled up. "I mean, for me they weren't. I guess I shouldn't assume I know the lives of all third graders, though. . . ."

Just play along, Millie. Don't act weird.

They got onto the bus and shared a seat for the first time. Of course they'd only been going to school together for a few days, but seat sharing was a big deal. Millie was suddenly worried about her breath from that protein bar and not feeling one hundred percent confident that she'd put on deodorant.

"Spelling tests can be hard." Millie said the first thing that came to her mind.

Then it was quiet between them. Millie was so focused on the fact that they'd all gotten the same fortunes this morning she was sort of unable to focus on anything else.

"Ah." Rodge nodded. "True."

"Was the pandemic hard for you?" Millie asked because it was all she could think of to say.

"Yeah, super hard. My dad lost all his work—he was a waiter at this super fancy, like corporate type restaurant that was totally shut down for months and then when it opened, they didn't have money to pay him. So, yeah." Rodge paused. "Let's not talk about it now, k?"

"K."

Millie knew better than to ask what his mom did because he obviously didn't want to talk about it. She also knew better than to ask how his school handled everything. She figured there had to be other schools that suffered like Shire, and never fully found their way out of it. But she didn't know any off the top of her head, and that made her feel lonely.

For some people they were able to just go back to their school, pretty much the way it had been. They had backyards to hang out in when it was dangerous to be inside with people.

It wasn't like that for people in cities.

Sometimes, Millie felt like no one really understood any of that. Well, nobody except Nora and Bea. But she'd never had a chance to really discuss it with them, anyway.

But maybe they'd be able to make sense of it all.

Maybe they'd find their way back to Shire. Even if it was just for one afternoon, to celebrate all the Shire awesomeness.

And being back together with Nora and Bea, especially back there, that made her feel like she was about to burst into the sky.

CHAPTER 24

Bea

AFTER DINNER, BEA'S PHONE RANG. It was an unknown number, but she answered it anyway.

"Hello?"

"Bea, it's Ms. Steinhauer." She paused. "Is this a good time to chat?"

"Yes, definitely! Hi!"

"Sooooo," Ms. Steinhauer said, and Bea's heart pounded. She couldn't tell much by the tone of her voice. "I'll get right to it. Good news and bad news." She paused again. "Mr. Hidgur gave us the go-ahead for this event. But in order for it to be the way you want it—it has to be next Saturday. We have a street closure permit in place next week for an event we're no longer having—you know our beloved Fall Fair—and he wants us to take advantage of it. It'll be hard to get another street permit anyway, so . . ."

Bea knew that closing a street in Manhattan was a huge deal and it took forever to get permits. Her mom had run the Fall Fair at Shire for many, many years and she always grumbled and complained about what a hassle it was: meetings and paperwork and no-parking signs and endless logistics.

"Okay!" Bea said. "We can do that."

"So I can't promise it'll be super well-attended, but Ms. Yanin in the development office will reach out to alumni, and we'll see how it goes. We'll have fun. Mr. Hidgur doesn't want it to be a fundraiser, just a time to really be together and focus on joy."

Bea's heart pounded and a thousand thoughts swirled around her brain. This was happening, and it was happening next week. They needed food, they needed people, they needed speakers and music and all the things.

Would anyone come?

Would any of this make a difference?

She had absolutely no idea.

As soon as Bea got off the phone with Ms. Steinhauer, she FaceTimed Nora and Millie.

They answered right away.

"It's happening."

"It is?" Millie shrieked. "For real?"

Bea nodded. "Yes. In one week, though. That's all the time we have."

"One week?" Nora asked. "What? How on earth?"

"Okay." Bea took a deep breath and exhaled. She curled up in a ball in the corner of her bed. "We can do this. We'll tell everyone we can. They'll post on Shire's social media. Maybe we can get the food donated from the Mansion? I bet Fiona, the best waitress in the world, can hook us up."

"Ooh, good idea," Millie chimed in.

Bea kept talking, "I mean, let's be honest, this isn't going to be the best planned event ever, but we'll get people there, and hopefully it'll be a nice day. And we'll bring all the fortune tellers . . . and maybe people will buy them and we'll donate the money . . ."

She was out of breath, but she'd made her point. Nora and Millie were silent, sort of staring at her, so she realized she needed to continue.

"Mills, you contact Fiona. You were the one closest to her, right?"

Millie nodded.

"Nor, maybe you can reach out to that kid Brendan, his family owned that party store? Maybe he can donate balloons."

"Oh, good idea. I can do that." Nora smiled.

"I'll make sure all logistics are taken care of on Shire's end, and promotion and tables and all of that . . ." Bea paused. "Do we need music?"

Bea didn't want to admit it, but she was mega overwhelmed. This felt like a huge undertaking, even if they had a year to do it. But one week? That was honestly impossible.

"We can make a playlist and get speakers," Nora said. "I bet the school has some."

"Good point."

Bea looked away from the screen and out the window. Her heart pounded and her first thought was to cancel this whole thing. It was too much to do in too short of a time period. Plus, what was the point? The school wasn't going to be saved. . . .

She felt hopeless and she wasn't even sure why.

They were so close to being back to normal and they had come so far, and all Bea wanted to do was give up.

She didn't understand herself at all.

The conversation spun around in circles after that and she listened and nodded but didn't offer any more suggestions. It was mostly just Millie and Nora saying how excited they were, and how thinking about this event, and being friends again, made everything else seem possible.

Bea wanted to feel that way. She'd felt that way before.

But now she was consumed with panic.

Nothing but panic.

CHAPTER 25

Nora

"YOU'RE OBSESSED WITH THIS AND you're ignoring us and ignoring Jeremy and we are so not into it," Esme said, plopping down on Nora's couch after school a few days later. "All you can think about is this event at your old school and it's super weird."

Nora sighed. She'd been expecting this. Esme and Jade had given her such an attitude at lunch today and they kept saying they'd explain later, and then she thought she was in the clear when she walked home alone, but no. Too good to be true.

Jade and Esme showed up at her door while she was halfway through her bag of pretzels and an episode of *Cake Wars*.

"I'm not obsessed and I'm not ignoring you," Nora said flatly, getting up to go to the pantry so she could put out some snacks. They were mad at her, yes, but that didn't mean she couldn't be a good host.

"Liar!" Jade said so loud it was practically a scream.

When Nora got back with the snacks, Jade and Esme were sprawled out on her couch—feet up and everything—staring at their phones. Maybe they weren't mad anymore and had already moved on?

That was her hope, because she had stuff to do. Nora wanted to reach out to Brendan to ask for donated decorations. She also wanted to text as many people as possible about it, and see if her mom could email all the parents of Penelope's grade.

Nora really didn't have time to delay on any of this.

She ran up to her room and dug her hand deep into the fortune teller box. She'd forgotten to take one this morning and the day had felt a little shaky ever since.

P-U-R-P-L-E

T-H-R-E-E

C-O-Y-O-T-E

Eyes on the prize. Always and forever. Eyes on the prize.

Her eyes were most certainly on that prize.

When Nora got back downstairs, Esme and Jade were in the same position she'd left them in; they hadn't touched any of the snacks. But Jeremy was there now, too, and this kid who everyone called Zander, and CJ from up the block. Nora didn't really know Zander and CJ well even though they always seemed to hang around with Jeremy. *As much as I tried to avoid him, he always seems to find his way back to me,* Nora thought. *Not sure why I want to avoid him so badly, but I just do.*

"We took matters into our own hands," Jade said, finally grabbing a handful of pretzels. "We all have boy-friends now, and we're all going to do couple-y things all the time. We're in seventh grade and this is how it is."

"Um." Nora crinkled her eyebrows and stared at Jeremy. She wasn't sure how on board with this he was, and she kind of wanted a private moment or two to discuss it with him. Also, she needed them to leave. She had way more important things to do.

"Um?" Esme said, mocking Nora.

"Um, that sounds great!" Nora said, one hundred percent enthusiastic-sounding. As ridiculous as it sounded, she had a feeling this was the quickest way to get rid of them. Maybe it wasn't great long-term, but it was what she needed to do right now.

Eyes on the prize.

"It sounds so great, actually," she continued. "But can we agree that we're all couples now and it's ah-mazing but also I need to take care of some stuff, so can we pick up with this tomorrow?"

"Huh?" CJ asked, totally tuned out and way more

focused on whatever game he was playing on his phone.

"CJ, come back to my house," Esme said. "My dad's out tonight and we can order Chinese. My sister will be home but she's chill."

CJ shrugged. "Okay, I gotta let my mom know, though. You know how it is. Moms."

Jade and Esme looked at one another—communicating with only their eyeballs. Nora wasn't totally sure what that was about, but she figured there was no way Esme was allowed to have boys over without a parent home, and probably that CJ wasn't even allowed to go over there. But hard to say.

Jade nudged Zander. "Want to walk to Nick's?" she asked.

He shrugged like he didn't care either way. "Yeah. I'm hungry."

Nora looked over at the table full of snacks, and felt a little defeated that her pretzels weren't good enough. But she had bigger fish to fry at the moment.

"K, great! Thanks for coming, everyone."

Then she noticed Jeremy still on the couch, looking confused.

"Jer, I'll call you later," she said, trying to be casual and sweet at the same time. "I'll explain."

He got up then and gave her a quick hug goodbye and within minutes, everyone was out of her house.

* * *

Nora was in the middle of writing an email to Brendan when a new text message popped up.

From Quinn.afisch@icloud.com.

Her heart pounded.

I heard you're planning a thing for Shire. Is everyone invited?

Nora couldn't believe it. The girl who was so exclusive she ripped apart a group of friends now wondered if everyone was invited. Nora wanted to say, *Yes, everyone is invited. Everyone except you.*

But she wouldn't do that.

But Nora realized she didn't need to respond right away. She could let Quinn sit with the discomfort for a bit. That feeling of knowing something was going on and not knowing if you were included or a part of it. Pretty much the worst feeling in the world. The feeling Quinn had made so many people experience, especially Millie.

She was getting a taste of her own medicine now.

Nora emailed Brendan and then her phone started buzzing with a FaceTime call.

It was Jeremy.

"Hey," she answered. "Sorry about before. I was just feeling overwhelmed."

"It's cool," Jeremy said. "Listen, about that whole boyfriend/girlfriend thing . . . we don't have to, like, do that. I mean, if you don't want to . . ."

"Oh, um." Nora looked away from the screen. She wasn't sure what he was saying. "Sometimes Jade and Esme just get kinda intense, and . . . yeah."

"Yeah, I agree." Jeremy smiled. "So . . ."

"So, let's just like leave it as whatever it is," Nora said, not sure what she was really saying anymore.

"Yeah, cool."

Then there was silence on FaceTime and then Nora said, "Listen, Jeremy. We're all good. I gotta run, though, k? I'll call you later."

"K, cool."

Nora had no idea what to make of any of this, and if she was honest with herself, she really didn't even want a boyfriend.

She FaceTimed Millie and Bea to tell them about the text.

"Um, hi," Nora said as soon as their faces popped onto the screen. "You'll never guess who texted me about Celebrate Shire."

Nora wondered if she was the only one who was officially calling it that. It had a perfect ring to it, though, and it was going to catch on.

"Ummmmm." Bea rolled her lips together.

"Quinn Afisch," Millie said flatly.

"Wow. Ding ding ding." Nora laughed.

"Of course she'd hear about it," Millie said. "Even now it's like she needs to be in the middle of everything."

Okay, so clearly, Millie was still bitter about the whole thing.

"Anyway," Nora said. "I'll write her back and tell her some of the details. Everyone's included!"

"Okay, great," Millie said, with the slightest of eye rolls. "So I have to tell you about this family here . . ."

"Yeah?" Bea asked.

She seemed distracted, typing on her laptop while FaceTiming. Nora didn't know what that was about.

"It's a long story," Millie answered. "I mean, it's not like bad and they're not, like, making trouble or anything. It's this whole food insecurity thing."

Nora and Bea were silent.

"Do you know what I mean?" Millie asked, sounding sort of confused that they hadn't answered her.

"Um, yeah, kind of," Bea said. "Can you explain more or is it really private?"

Millie hesitated to answer. Nora wasn't sure if she wanted to or not or if she felt like she was being put on the spot, but she'd been the one to bring it up in the first place.

"So they just moved here. And I didn't realize it right away but my dad had applied for some grant to have some of the cabins and cottages be for low-income families. . . ." She sighed. "Anyway, and this one family got it, and is living here indefinitely, but they can't afford food and my mom goes with the mom to the food pantry and she tries to help."

"Okay, go on." Nora smiled. "We're listening."

"So one of the brothers in the family, Roger but he goes by Rodge, he's our age. Anyway, Rodge and I have become friends, and, um, maybe, like more than friends." She face-palmed herself and Nora figured Millie regretted bringing it up. "Back to that later, but anyway, it's just making things weird between us because he thinks I don't understand, and obviously I don't totally understand but I want to." She shut her eyes tight for a second or two and then opened them again. "Anyway, it's just a lot."

Nora realized Millie said *anyway* a lot. Had she always done that? Was it a new thing? She wasn't sure. They felt so close and so far away at the same time.

"That sounds really hard, Mills." Bea bit her bottom lip. "I think just being there for him and asking questions and trying to understand is all you can do."

Millie nodded. "I think he assumes we're rich. And I mean, hello? We are so not rich."

"Yeah, I mean, you're not." Nora clenched her teeth, realizing that may have been rude. "I mean, it's okay. Neither are we. But yeah."

That was definitely NOT the thing to say, Nora thought. *I wish I could take it back.*

"So I don't know. It's a lot of things. But I need to go find him and talk to him now, I think . . ."

"Okay, well, go go. I need to finish this email to Brendan and write back to Quinn . . ."

"Good luck, lovies." Bea smiled. "Talk later."

They hung up and Nora realized she knew so little about what Bea's life was like right now. She knew a little about Millie's—this kid Rodge and running the lake community and stuff. But Bea? No clue. Maybe it was because Bea was always the most secretive of the three? Or did Bea not have much going on right now?

That didn't make sense.

Nora finished her email to Brendan, asking if he could donate stuff from the party store for Celebrate Shire. And then she finally wrote back to Quinn.

Yup. Celebrate Shire. A chance for all of us to come back together. Finally! Come!

Quinn wrote back a second later. *Kk I'll ask my mom.*

Nora stared at her phone for a moment or two longer, debating what else to say, and then she realized there wasn't anything else to say.

She thought about something she'd never thought of before then. Or maybe she had thought about it but she'd forgotten.

Did Quinn even know what that whole thing with her birthday invitations did? Did she know the damage it did to Nora, Bea, and Millie's friendship? And would telling her have made a difference?

Deep in thought again for the millionth time that day, Nora rubbed her temples and fell back onto her bed, quickly drifting off to sleep.

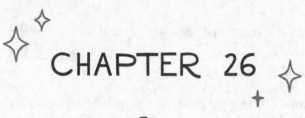

CHAPTER 26

Bea

"I STILL CAN'T BELIEVE YOU'RE doing this," Danny said to Bea at breakfast the next morning. "And I still can't believe you didn't even get caught faking sick and going alone all the way to Shire on orientation day. . . ."

"You've said this so many times already, Danny." Bea paused. "Leave it alone, okay? Don't come. Whatever."

"Oh, I'm coming! I'm gonna help!" Danny said forcefully. "All of my friends are coming, too. We want to see what this is all about."

"Good," Bea replied.

A few moments later, Mom and Aunt Claire came downstairs. Their mom looked probably the most disheveled Bea had ever seen her.

"Mom?" She looked up at her, heart pounding. "Are you okay?"

"No." She pulled out a chair for Aunt Claire, got her to sit down, and then rushed around the kitchen like she was searching for three thousand things at the same time.

"What's going on?" Bea got up and walked over to the fridge to stand next to her mom. "Tell me, Mom. I'm worried."

"Aunt Claire's seizures. Nonstop. We were up all night." She shook her head. "Seems like we can never catch a break. I got her a last-minute appointment today but I'm missing work again. Dad's away. Again." She sighed. "Let me just do what I need to do, Bea. Okay?"

Bea nodded, and shuffled back to the table to finish her bowl of cereal. It felt like a cinder block was sitting somewhere between her chin and her stomach.

She forced herself to finish breakfast and brought her bowl over to the sink, and that's when Sam burst through their kitchen door and somehow launched herself next to Bea.

"Um, hi?" Bea said.

"You're ignoring me and I'm over it." She turned around to face Bea's mom, Aunt Claire, and Danny at the table. "You all should know that Bea's ignoring me. Complete ghosting. I tried to really welcome her to Prenner and she doesn't even care."

Bea felt like she was in a nightmare and she was hoping she would wake up any second. No one actually showed up at someone else's house. Yet Sam seemed to do it kind of often. Here she was, right now, in her kitchen before eight in the morning.

"Sam, let's go outside, or actually, let's just head to school. We can talk on the way." Bea shut the dishwasher door, grabbed her hoodie and backpack off the hook, and just started to leave the house, assuming Sam would follow her.

This was not how she wanted to start the day.

No one really said goodbye to Bea, but she figured they were all as equally flabbergasted by this whole thing as she was. Moments later, Bea and Sam were outside.

"I can't take you anymore," Sam said. "You were my friend and now you're not and I have to open up and ask why. I don't play these on-again, off-again friendship games. It's happened to me so many times with friends at Prenner and at camp and I thought things were different with you."

Bea swallowed hard. She hadn't expected this. Sam seeming vulnerable and shaky and sad?

This is weird, Bea thought. Sam was the confident one. The tough one. The girl who seemed not to care about social hierarchies or anything at all.

"Just tell me you hate me and you don't want to be my friend and I'm not cool, and you only care about your Shire friends. Just say it to my face and I'll move on." Sam started crying. Bea had never seen Sam cry. Suddenly,

Bea felt like she understood approximately zero things about life and the world and friendship and pretty much anything.

"Sam," Bea said. "None of that is true."

"Then tell me why you avoid me, tell me why you never want to hang out and barely respond to my texts. Tell me why suddenly you seem to think I'm the worst person ever," Sam continued.

Her words felt like a million tacks being poked into Bea's palm.

"I'm just distracted, Sam," Bea said finally. "And, like, honestly, I thought you didn't really like me, like you only hung out with me because you felt bad for me."

"Stop. You're lying."

"I'm not!" Bea yelled. "I thought you had a crush on Danny, too, and that's why you hung out with me."

"Well, everyone has a crush on Danny," Sam admitted.

"Okay, well, ew." Bea laughed, because it was honestly funny to her that everyone loved her brother, but she also wanted to break up the tension. "Seriously, though, Sam. I don't hate you, and I'm glad you spoke up. I'm distracted now with this event we're planning for Shire, but it'll be over in less than a week. And then I'll be a better friend to you."

"Promise?" Sam asked.

"Promise."

There's a whole other side of Sam I never knew was there.

At all. Is that the secret of friendship, actually? Bea wondered. Maybe you can never really be that close to someone until you open up to them.

Maybe if Millie and Nora and me had actually talked about *y* things were changing and maybe we weren't so into the *f* *ne* tellers anymore, and also talked about the Quinn Afisch *i* *nt* instead of just getting angry, we could have avoided all the heartache that went along with it.

"I'm glad you said something, Sam." Bea looked over at her as they walked the rest of the way to school.

Sam shrugged. "I'm not good at talking about this stuff, either, you know."

"Do you think anyone is?" Bea asked.

"Probably not, but I've had too many friendships just evaporate and disappear and it all feels terrible and painful, and I just couldn't handle another situation like that." She looked over at Bea. "Plus, I see actual friend potential in you, so I figured it was really worth saying something."

Bea smiled. "I see friend potential in you, too."

For the first time, she actually meant it.

CHAPTER 27

Millie

"DO YOU GUYS EVEN REALIZE that we're seeing each other tomorrow?" Millie asked Bea and Nora on FaceTime that night. "Like in person!"

"I don't think I realize it," Bea replied. "Honestly. Like I know we are, but it hasn't really sunk in yet."

"Me neither. Exactly. This whole thing feels fake," Nora added.

"What if we get there and the street's not closed? Or no one shows up or the food doesn't arrive or any and all of the above plus three million other things to worry about?" Millie asked, sitting on her hands to avoid biting her nails.

"Mills, stop." Nora shook her head. "We need to have faith. We've done all we can do. It'll be what it can be.

No matter what, we'll see each other. THAT IS WHAT MATTERS MOST IN THE WHOLE ENTIRE WORLD!" she screamed, and then laughed at herself. "Also, we're bringing people together."

"She's right," Bea added.

Millie's stomach rumbled. She realized she was hungry and that she should've eaten dinner but her mom had made meat loaf and she hated meat loaf. So instead she had packed up the leftovers and brought it over to Rodge.

He didn't seem thrilled with it, either. Turned out he also hated meat loaf.

"Rodge still thinks he's a charity case," Millie announced. "There seems to be no way I can convince him otherwise. I don't know what to do."

"Can we table everything not related to Celebrate Shire until after Celebrate Shire?" Bea asked. "Honestly, my brain can only handle so much."

"Same," Nora answered. "And I have a lot to tell you guys."

"Well, now we need to know!" Millie shrieked.

"Tabling everything!" Bea sang, her eyes wide. "Sheesh, people. Sheesh."

There were moments when things felt okay between the three of them, but then moments like this where it all still felt forced.

Maybe tomorrow—being back in person together—would really make things feel normal again.

They spent the rest of the call going over the logistics. Bea, Danny, and their mom (plus Aunt Claire because she couldn't stay alone) would get there first. Their dad was away. Of course he was.

Then Millie would arrive whenever she could with the rest of her family, but since they were traveling from the Berkshires, around three hours away, they weren't entirely sure when they'd get there. Millie's dad put Carl, the handyman, in charge for the day, and they were all hoping for the best.

Nora, Penelope, and their mom would come as early as possible. The drive from Tressdale was only forty minutes or so, but traffic was always uncertain.

The three girls all wanted to get there early to set up and welcome everyone and of course reunite in person. Hug and screech and whatever else seventh-grade friends did when they reunited after almost two years apart.

Not having Bea and Nora these past few years had led Millie to question everything. She didn't really know who she was. She sort of felt like mostly everyone met her and instantly hated her. She found herself in an unknown place, with zero friends.

Nothing at all felt safe and secure.

And now they were talking again, but could she trust it? Would it last? Millie had no idea.

It was hard to let herself feel comfortable when it seemed like everything was on such shaky ground, so uncertain.

CHAPTER 28

Bea

BEA, DANNY, THEIR MOM, AND Aunt Claire left their house at seven in the morning so they could be at Shire at eight. The school maintenance guys had helped hang the *No Parking* flyers and when they arrived, the street was barricaded off and by some miracle, everyone had actually moved their cars.

Maybe things are going to go okay, maybe even better than okay, Bea thought, taking the empty street as a good sign. Plus the sun was shining and it was a perfect fall Saturday and she was going to be reunited with Millie and Nora soon.

This day was full of possibilities.

As soon as she got off the subway, she pulled a fortune teller out of her pocket. The one she'd opened this morning at home felt a little vague. The fortune was *everyone loves you*, which was nice and all but also not much of a fortune.

She needed some extra reassurance.

B-L-U-E

F-R-O-G

T-H-R-E-E

You are making things happen!

"Is that Bea Grellick?" one of the maintenance guys yelled out as soon as they were walking up Eighty-Seventh Street. "And Danny Grellick, too!"

She beamed. For that split second, Bea felt like a celebrity. She looked over at Danny, wondering if he felt the same, but she wasn't even sure he was paying attention.

"It is!" Bea and Danny's mom yelled back like she was their manager or something, and then Bea's pride of feeling like a celebrity dissipated and she felt more mortified by her mother.

Good things could only last for so long, she reasoned.

"Oh, Bea." Danny shook his head. "What have you gotten us into? I could be on the couch playing video games right now, and here I am . . . um, I don't even know what I'm doing."

Bea ignored his negativity, plus she knew it wasn't

entirely true. There was a part of him that was excited. "You're going to pick up the food donations. And you're going now."

They kept walking the rest of the way up the street until they reached Shire's majestic red doors. Bea felt an achy nostalgia, a longing, a deep wish in the core of her soul to go back to school at Shire. Maybe even in kindergarten, to start all over again.

She looked over at Aunt Claire, wanting to remind her of the time she'd come to visit Bea's class in first grade on special visitors day, but it was clear she was already in the middle of one of her silent types of seizures.

And maybe Bea's mom was swept up in the being-back-at-Shire moment because she was barely paying attention.

"Mom!" Bea yelled, her heart pounding. "Aunt Claire! She's about to fall over."

"Oh my goodness!" her mom shrieked, and carefully whisked her over to one of the chairs that was already outside. The Shire maintenance guys had already done a great job setting up tables with chairs around them and tablecloths and everything. Bea was kind of surprised that so much had been done already.

Luckily, Aunt Claire made it to a chair in time, and she sat down. When she came out of the seizure, she looked around. No clue where she was.

"Momo?" she asked.

"I'm here, Clairey," Bea's mom said, and sighed.

Bea sighed too. She loved Aunt Claire. But she resented her a bit also. Was she going to have seizures this whole day? Her mom wouldn't have a chance to talk to any Shire friends or even enjoy herself because she'd be so focused on Aunt Claire.

Maybe it was a mistake to bring her here, but she'd been having so many seizures lately, she couldn't be left alone.

"Bea," her mom said, walking over to her. When she got there, she put her hands on Bea's shoulders and pulled her close. "I just want to say thank you for helping look out for Aunt Claire, and loving her so much." She paused, and Bea could tell she was trying as hard as she could not to start sobbing in the middle of Eighty-Seventh Street. "And I'm sorry I'm distracted. I'm sorry you don't feel like a priority. I am going to do better. I promise."

Bea nodded. "I love you, Mom. Thank you."

Buoyed by that short chat with her mom, Bea walked into Shire with a new confidence. She wanted to find Ms. Steinhauer and thank her for all the help. And she wanted to look around school a little, too.

The school was eerily quiet, which made sense since it was a Saturday, but Ms. Steinhauer had said she'd be there. Of course she would! This was all thanks to her efforts—finding the fortune tellers, sending them to the girls, and even helping to organize Celebrate Shire.

Shire wouldn't be Shire without Ms. Steinhauer, and this day would definitely not be possible or happening without her.

Bea went right up to the third floor to Ms. Steinhauer's classroom. The lights were off. It was empty. Walls were bare. Desks all pushed together in one corner. Nothing on the bulletin boards.

The clock above the door sounded louder than it had ever sounded before. Probably because the school—and the classroom—were so quiet.

"Ms. Steinhauer?" Bea called out softly.

No response.

Bea couldn't believe how different the room seemed, even from the last time she was here, which was only a little over a week ago. Of course it was way different from when Bea was in Ms. Steinhauer's class in third grade, probably the best year of her life.

But now? This felt like an abandoned classroom, somewhere students learned years ago. It seemed like it should be covered in layers and layers of dust.

There wasn't much time to linger in here because Bea had to get outside and help with the setup, see if Nora and Millie were here already. She knew all of that. But then she remembered something. Something major.

The markers! she shouted inside her head. *They were here! We left them here!*

Way at the end of the hall was a closet that used to

have extremely organized shelves. One was for board games, one was for puzzles, one was for paper, and one was for pencils and markers and crayons.

The students were always allowed to be in and out of that closet during Choice Time, as long as they promised to keep it tidy and put everything away when they were done.

Usually all went well and the kids followed through with their promise.

Except for one day when the classroom turned to mayhem.

Jake Manaforte got into a fight with Desmond Craig. Juliet Lufel got into a fight with the twins Rebel and Jaime. Ms. Steinhauer kept having to separate kids and get involved, and pretty soon it was time to get to lunch, and everything was still all over the place.

Bea, Millie, and Nora had looked at one another. They never admitted it out loud, but they'd been waiting for a time like this. A chance for them to offer to put everything away so they'd have access to the closet without anyone else there, and they could get to the little secret cabinet they'd found at the back and hide away their magic markers and the rules they'd made up for the fortune tellers to keep them consistent.

Not hidden away forever, of course, just until the next Choice Time, only transported to their homes on weekends and school breaks, rotating from one home to the other, carefully following the calendar they'd set for them.

The goal was to move them as little as possible so they wouldn't get lost in transit. The *Write Your Destiny* markers had to be kept safe and accounted for one hundred percent of the time.

When you come across magical markers, you don't take that for granted. You protect them with all that you have.

But when Shire closed because of the pandemic, and the girls were in a fight, all of that was forgotten and the markers were left behind.

Bea opened the closet door and it creaked the way it always did. She whipped around, certain someone had heard that and would appear.

But nope. No one was there.

The shelves were empty now—of course they were—the whole floor was empty. But the little door at the bottom that they'd discovered was a hidden cabinet was very easy to find this way. Bea turned around one more time to be certain she was alone and then she looked at her watch and realized she needed to be outside. She had to do this quickly.

Bea grabbed on to the little cabinet doorknob and pulled it open and there it was: the pink shoebox from Millie's beloved patent leather Mary Janes.

"Bea!"

She whipped around and saw Nora and Millie standing there. She froze in place.

"We knew we'd find you here," Nora said, and it was so casual-sounding, it was as if the three of them had been together the day before.

Bea stared at them, unable to speak. They were so much taller; it was hard to tell that on FaceTime since they were always sitting down. Every single thing about them was different, it seemed!

She walked over to them, and spread out her arms, and pulled them into the tightest group hug in the history of group hugs. Tears streamed down her face. Even when the hug was over, Bea still found herself unable to speak.

She'd known how much she missed them, but it wasn't until right at that very moment that she actually felt how extreme it was, how unbelievably lost she was without them.

She'd sort of gotten used to it—but now that they were right there in front of her, it was as if every moment she'd spent missing them was piled on top of each other and she realized she missed them the most anyone could ever miss another person.

"Guys!" she said finally. "And I know we're not supposed to say *guys* anymore, but still. "You guys. I cannot believe this. Can you?"

"What exactly are you referring to?" Millie asked.

"Because I'd say all of it is pretty hard to believe."

They laughed.

"We are reunited," Nora squealed. "With each other. And with the *Write Your Destiny* markers!"

"Are we spooked that the fortune tellers turned weird, and I guess, like, magical, when we were apart . . . ?" Millie mused. "They were normal and goofy when we made them, right? Not sure what that means."

"It means that the magic was in place to actually bring us back together!" Nora yelped. "I mean, hello?"

"But wait." Bea sat down, suddenly overwhelmed. "That means that the universe or whatever knew all along we'd break apart somehow? And so that's why we found the markers and made the rules and the fortunes in the first place, because even though we were destined to break apart, we were also destined to come back together?"

"Maybe?" Millie shrugged. "We can sort all of that out later. Let's just get the shoebox!"

Nora and Bea nodded and Bea grabbed the shoebox again, and hid it away under her sweatshirt in her backpack like she'd done before.

"K, let's go!" Bea said. "Has anyone seen Ms. Steinhauer, by the way?"

"Yeah, she's outside," Nora answered. "She was looking for you, and when you weren't out on the street we said we had an idea of where you were. . . ."

Bea smiled.

It hadn't been her plan to go straight to the closet and find the markers. But it did settle on her brain soon after getting to Shire. They understood her impatience, how curiosity always got the best of her.

That was the thing about real, true, lifelong friends. They'd always know you, no matter what. They'd know the foods you hated and if you ran cold or hot. They'd know if you had a weird middle name or a nickname only your mom called you. They'd know if you preferred body wash or bar soap (ew) and if you showered in the morning or at night.

They knew all the things, and even if time passed or fights happened or Quinn Afisch's birthday party invitations broke a trio of fifth graders apart, they'd still know all of it. Probably forever.

"Is Quinn Afisch here?" Bea asked, swallowing hard when they were almost out of the Shire building and out onto the street.

"Not that we saw." Millie shook her head. "We would have warned you."

They knew things like that, too. Even after so much time had passed, they still knew things like that.

It's pretty miraculous actually, Bea thought.

The three girls, best friends since kindergarten, with only a one-and-a-half-year hiatus in their friendship, walked out onto Eighty-Seventh Street, ready to throw a party for their beloved school.

Celebrate Shire, it was called. But deep down in Bea's heart and soul, she wished it were called The Event That Will Definitely Save Shire. Maybe somehow, it would be.

She'd commute from Kensington; she didn't care. She'd convince Nora to commute from Tressdale and maybe Millie could take turns staying at each of their homes during the school year.

Bea would do whatever it took for Shire to still be Shire and for the three of them to be in seventh grade together.

It seemed close to impossible, but when she pictured it in her head, and had a fortune teller in her hand, there was always a tiny, minuscule glimmer of hope.

CHAPTER 29

Nora

QUINN AFISCH WAS STANDING RIGHT outside Shire's front entrance, waiting for Bea, Millie, and Nora as soon as they left the building.

"Um, hi?" she sang, like she was waiting for a gigantic greeting.

"Um, hi?" Nora sang right back. Even though she had actually been the one invited to Quinn's fifth-grade party, the "coolest" one of the trio, right now her insides felt a combination of sour and maybe on the verge of being on fire.

"You guys really organized this? Like the whole thing?" Quinn asked.

Nora was sort of surprised that she was just jumping to the present day, present moment. Like, shouldn't she want to know what had happened in the past one and a half years—where they'd gone, if they were still friends, why'd they left Shire, all of the above.

"We did." Millie fake-smiled. Nora knew all of Millie's smiles, and she had a lot of them. Her wide-eyed, true, joyful smile, her sort of lopsided one when she was confused, her closed-mouth one when she was insecure, and then this one—her toothy, over-the-top fake one.

"Wow, I'm impressed. I mean, food donations from Tal's Bagels, Kobe sushi, Italian Village? The Mansion! I mean, wow. Just wow." She paused. "Sooooo, whatcha been up to since the end of fifth grade?"

Millie, Nora, and Bea looked at one another.

Where to start? Nora thought to herself.

But then Bea jumped in. "Well, since this is starting— I'll give you the quick version." She paused. "Ready?"

"Um, I think so?" Quinn laughed.

Nora had forgotten what an annoying laugh she had.

"I moved to Kensington, in Brooklyn. I go to Prenner Collegiate, it's fine, nothing like Shire, but fine. Millie lives in the Berkshires, and Nora lives in the suburbs." She shrugged.

"Tressdale," Nora added. "In Westchester."

"Oh. Nice." It seemed like Quinn didn't know what to say after that. "I'm sure you all know what happened to me?"

They shook their heads. They had no idea.

Quinn looked off into the distance. "Oh, I just figured,

I mean . . . I don't know."

Nora knew what she was trying to say—that everyone was obsessed with her and cared where she moved and what happened to her. It wasn't true. Not at all.

Quinn continued, "I had to move to Vermont. My mom got remarried. My stepdad is a huge jerk, and now I have twin stepbrothers who torture me constantly."

Millie, Nora, and Bea all made over-the-top sad faces.

"That sounds hard," Nora added. "Anyway, we need to go set up. Want to come help, or . . ." Her voice trailed off, and she instantly regretted inviting her. Bea and Millie were going to be mad. But what was that Gandhi quote everyone loved? *Be the change you want to see in the world?* Well, she was doing just that. Quinn was exclusive, and mean, and had broken up friendships because of her stupid birthday party.

But Nora was going to set things right, and include her now. Sure, it was just down the street to put out some napkins and plates, and fill some of those giant Gatorade jugs of water, but still.

An invite was an invite.

"Seriously?" Quinn chirped. "Yes! I'd love to help."

The four girls walked down Eighty-Seventh Street together and got to the food table, and they carefully put out the plates and cups and everything. Danny and a few of his Shire friends were arriving with the food donations, and the music was playing, and all the remaining

Shire faculty was outside, smiling, chatting. *Schmoozing*, as Nora's mom often said.

"Can I just admit something?" Quinn asked, putting out a few stacks of red cups. At least this time it sounded like she was asking a question when she was actually asking a question.

Nora nodded, and then Millie and Bea did, too.

"I always wanted to be friends with you guys," she said softly. "The three of you were, like, the example of friendship for me. Even now, in Vermont, I've tried really hard to find girls to be in a trio with."

"Really?" Millie asked, shocked. "But what about Courtney, Brooke, Amabelle, and Hilary? Your whole crew."

Nora looked at her. It didn't surprise her that Millie still knew the names of Quinn's fifth-grade best friends, and could recall them out of the blue like this.

"They were fine, but not always nice to me."

Bea stared at Quinn, and Nora's stomach sank a little bit. She knew Bea was going to say something sort of blunt and intense.

"But you guys were considered the popular people or whatever back then?" Bea said, all matter-of-fact like there was absolutely no denying it.

Truthfully, Nora wasn't one hundred percent sure she agreed. Popularity was subjective. Why were popular people considered popular when only their own little clique liked them?

"Yeah, maybe," Quinn said, arranging the napkins into neat little piles. "But they weren't nice to me. I wanted to be friends with you guys," she repeated.

"Then why did you do that with your birthday party!" Millie yelled, and then quickly covered her mouth. "Sorry, I didn't mean to scream. But seriously, why did you do that?"

"Do what?" Quinn asked, biting the inside of her cheek.

Millie, Nora, and Bea stared at each other.

Had they imagined the whole thing? Was the Quinn Afisch incident not an incident at all?

No way. Nora knew it was.

Nora knew it because she was the one who was invited, the one who went along with it and didn't speak up about the way Quinn had asked in front of people who she wasn't inviting. Nora didn't stand up for her friends. She still felt guilty about it. About all of it.

"You went around asking people for their parents' info in front of people you weren't inviting, Quinn," Nora said softly, her words coming out scratchy and weak. "You made it clear who was and who wasn't invited. You only asked for mine, and not Bea's or Millie's. And by the way, there's a Shire directory. There has always been a Shire directory."

Quinn was quiet.

"Do you remember doing that?" Millie asked. "You *have* to remember."

Bea looked back and forth at all of them. "It tore apart our friendship."

Nora gasped, covering her mouth, sort of shocked Bea had said that and feeling the sting of the experience all over again, like it was almost happening right now.

"It did?" Quinn sniffled. "I guess, um, yeah. I do remember it."

She sat down on the curb behind one of the food tables and started sobbing. Nora, Bea, and Millie looked at one another in a *now what* kind of way, and Nora realized they had to go sit with her, and comfort her. This was seriously slowing down their set-up time, but thankfully the Shire maintenance guys and whatever parents were there already were helping, too.

When Millie, Nora, and Bea sat down on the curb next to Quinn, she started talking a mile a minute, like all her thoughts were sweaters and she was wearing too many and had to take them off immediately, like she'd been waiting for a time when she could open up and get it out into the open.

"I know I did it. I don't know why I just pretended I didn't remember. I do remember. Of course I do." She paused, looking at the three of them. "I had no idea it broke apart your friendship, though, because school went remote and then we all moved away. . . ." She paused, and then started talking again. "I know why I did it, too. Because for the first time in my life, I felt like I was sort of the queen bee. My parents were getting divorced and they were both feeling super guilty and so they were letting me have this blowout birthday party with a DJ and sushi platters and all this stuff, but I couldn't invite the whole grade—there would never have been space in the party room in our building. . . ."

Nora didn't know why she was going into all this detail. Celebrate Shire was starting, and frankly, she didn't want to waste any more time on the Quinn Afisch incident.

Sure, it seemed like Quinn had grown up since fifth grade and maybe regretted the whole thing, but still.

Nora wanted to move on. Really, really badly.

"Girls!" Ms. Steinhauer appeared in front of them. "We're starting, right? Look how many people are here!"

They all stood up and looked around at their beloved Eighty-Seventh Street full of people.

"You did this!" she said, "You made this happen."

"Well, it wouldn't have if not for you, and finding the fortune tellers . . ." Millie stopped talking when she realized Quinn was still right there with them. She worried she'd have to get into the whole explanation of the fortune tellers and how it all started and all that had happened since they'd discovered the *Write Your Destiny* markers all those years ago.

But when Millie glanced over, Quinn was completely checked out, staring out into the street, tears streaming down her face. She wasn't paying attention to anything, and was clearly a puddle of emotion.

"Quinn, are you okay?" Ms. Steinhauer asked, noticing, too.

"Oh yeah." She shrugged. "Totally fine."

Ms. Steinhauer hesitated a moment, but then she said, "Well, let's go enjoy. Not sure why you're all hiding over here. . . ."

The girls all looked at one another and then burst into laughter. Even Quinn. Nora didn't think she had ever spent this much time with them before, and they definitely hadn't laughed together like this before.

It didn't matter.

Everything was upside down and wacky and nothing felt one hundred percent the way Nora had expected it to. Not even close, actually.

Quinn Afisch laughing with them? Spending time with them?

Sure. It was fine.

Everything was just fine.

CHAPTER 30

Millie

MILLIE COULDN'T BELIEVE THEY WERE there. It had been hours already and she still couldn't believe it. The three of them together again. *Okay, with Quinn Afisch, too, weird but whatever.* They were all there—walking in and out of Shire, eating bagels and pizza and cookies. Drinking iced tea and sitting on the curb. Dancing to "Story of My Life" and "Shake It Off" and all the songs on the playlist. They were chatting with teachers and parents, and answering the same questions over and over again.

"How did you do this?"

"What made you want to do this?"

"What do you miss the most about Shire?"

"Well, we miss everything, and we love Shire," Millie answered for the millionth time. "And we're sad about all

that's happened, and we want to, um, well celebrate it."
She giggled.

"You're wonderful," the woman replied. None of the girls knew who she was. Maybe someone's mom or grandma. Probably grandma. She looked older.

Quinn was off at the end of the street with her mom and some other people, and Nora, Bea, and Millie were eating doughnuts when a reporter approached them.

"I was told you're the girls who made this event happen," the woman said. "I'm Katie Follett, from ABC News. We heard about this event celebrating Shire, the oldest K-to-twelve coed school in Manhattan, and we just had to be here. . . ."

"Shire's the best," Nora said.

"Better than best," Bea added. "We miss it so much. We'd been here since kindergarten, but then the lower school closed after the pandemic, and . . ."

Millie looked over at her, scared she was saying too much, and this would be on TV and all of NYC, and maybe even the whole country, would see them.

"Why don't we focus on all the things you loved about Shire?" Katie Follett asked. "We'd love to elevate it. Seems like a really special place."

So the girls and Katie Follett sat down at one of the food tables and they listed all the things: the Fall Fair where the street was closed, just like it was today; bake sales, especially the Halloween one where all the parents dressed up; weekly parades celebrating everything from musical instruments to monarch butterflies to poems. Monarch butterflies! That all lower school kids got to take home a chrysalis every year. They went on and on. Autobiography presentations, churros for dessert, the Mister Softee truck on the last day of school, the teacher/student buddy program and the senior/kindergarten buddy program. The whole grade sleeping over together in the school gym, field trips to the Met, and even the chance to *be* a Met librarian for the weekly toddler story time. Answering the phone in the main office in fifth grade—for half the year, until Covid hit, at least. Student government, and a field day on Randall's Island, five-minute chats with Ms. Giroux, hallway birthday parties with singing and cheering and locker decorations, the fact that everyone's birthday was a Shire holiday. They went on and on. There were too many things to name.

Soon even Katie Follett was choked up. "Wow."

"Here's the main thing you need to know," Millie said. "At Shire, everyone felt like they were every teacher's favorite student. At Shire, everyone felt like they were the best at whatever they wanted to be the best at." She paused. "Because the teachers gave us the confidence to feel we could do *literally* anything."

By that point, it seemed that Katie Follett was speechless. The cameraperson was filming and Katie was just nodding.

"There are schools that are, like, more rigorous or whatever; I don't really know," Nora added. "But there's no other school like Shire. And that's why it's so sad that we lost it."

"Thank you so much for sharing this with me," Katie said finally, her voice scratchy.

Millie chewed on her pinkie nail even though she tried not to. Scared Katie would ask more questions that would lead them to bring up the fortune tellers, Millie tried to end the whole thing.

She didn't want to get into anything about that. It was too out there and spooky, and no one would get it anyway.

Most likely, no one would even believe them.

Fortunately, the interview ended after that. The girls' parents had to sign some kind of release, and the interview was maybe going to appear on the six o'clock news? No one was really sure what was happening.

Celebrate Shire was winding down—they were full from pizza and bagels and doughnuts and way too much iced tea, exhausted from all the emotional moments, and feeling slightly lighter after actually discussing the Quinn Afisch incident with Quinn Afisch.

"Party canoe and I love you, too! We haven't said that once today!" Nora screamed. "I can't even believe it!"

"Me neither." Bea shook her head.

Before everyone trickled out, Mr. Hidgur spoke in his

226

loudest voice and said, "Thank you all for coming today to celebrate Shire and share in the magic one more time. As you know, the future of the school is uncertain, along with most things in life, unfortunately." He paused. "But there's still a place for you here, and we hope you'll find your way back to us. Brighter days are on the horizon. To our beloved alumni, Bea, Millie, and Nora—thank you for making us realize that a day like this was possible. You are three of the reasons why Shire is the magical place that it was, that it is, and that it'll continue to be. Remember that magic, and take it with you wherever you go in life. Thank you again. Be well."

When cleanup was starting and the few remaining people were wandering around, chatting, Millie turned to Nora and Bea. "Let's go back inside to open the box, in Ms. Steinhauer's classroom where it all began, where we started making the fortune tellers." She was wide-eyed, like they were on the cusp of something extraordinary. "That's where we should be opening the box."

Nora nodded. "She's right. Come on."

So they all walked inside, and up the three flights of stairs, and found themselves back in Ms. Steinhauer's empty, lonely-feeling classroom.

Millie's phone buzzed with a text from her mom that they needed to get on the road and head back to the Berkshires soon to try to avoid traffic.

"We need to be quick," Millie announced, shocked

her friends were able to hear her over the sound of her pounding heart.

They opened the shoebox and found the markers in the plastic package that had *Write Your Destiny* across the front on huge curlicue letters. Millie wondered if they were all dried out by now.

And underneath: the rules for their magical fortune tellers.

Always start with your favorite color and then work backward to least favorite.

Include obscure animals when you can. Try not to use cats or dogs.

The fortunes should be quirky and silly and fun and sometimes make no sense AT ALL. NEVER TAKE THIS TOO SERIOUSLY.

We are writing people's destinies. THE MARKERS SAY SO. NEVER FORGET THAT.

N+B+M now and forever

"I really gotta go," Millie said, sniffling. "What's our main takeaway, literally and figuratively? And who is taking this box home, I guess is what I'm asking . . . ?"

"No one. Let's all take pictures of the rules," Nora demanded. "And we leave the box here."

"Really?" Bea asked.

"Really?" Millie repeated.

"Really," Nora answered. "We have time to figure all of this out."

Bea said, "But we don't know if the markers even write anymore, if they're all dried up, without ink. What do we do about that? Do we go back to making fortune tellers? Make it an online fundraiser?"

"All TBD," Nora said, matter-of-fact. "We have to leave them here. Because that gives us a definitive, super important, and necessary reason to come back."

Millie sighed. "She's right."

"What if someone finds them, though? The people renting the classrooms?" Millie asked, teeth clenched. "I don't know."

Nora answered, "No one's found them in all these years. I have faith. But even if someone did . . . maybe they'd take over what we started."

The three of them looked at one another. They took pictures of the markers and the rules, and about three dozen selfies. Millie put the cover back on the shoebox and Bea returned it to its secret spot in the hidden cabinet.

They hugged and cried and wiped their tears on the sleeves of their sweatshirts, and then they walked down the three flights of stairs, through Shire's iconic red doors, and out onto Eighty-Seventh Street.

"Millie, I'm sorry I was mean to you about the fortune tellers," Nora whispered as they huddled in a circle outside, arms over each other's shoulders. "They matter.

And you matter. And your feelings matter. And I am so sorry."

"I forgive you." Millie sniffled again.

"This isn't the end, you know," Bea said. "We'll be back."

"*We* already are back," Millie replied with a smile.

ACKNOWLEDGMENTS

Thank you, thank you, thank you to the lights and loves of my life: Dave, Aleah, Hazel, and Kibbitz. You inspire me and fill my days with happiness. Your support, patience, and, most of all, your love makes anything seem possible.

Hazel, thank you for reading an early draft of this book and giving me feedback!

To the Greenwald crew—David, Lauren, Lennie, Max, Shana, Bobbi, and Joey—thank you for being on my team, making me laugh, and caring about me.

To the Rosenbergs—Aaron, Karen, Ari, Aryn, Ezra, Maayan, Tavi, Henry, Elon, and Andrew—thanks for always asking how the writing is going and cheering me on.

Alyssa Eisner Henkin, I am endlessly appreciative for your steady guidance, wisdom, support, patience, and enthusiasm. Thank you for always supporting me and my writing.

Maria Barbo, thank you for believing in this book from the beginning.

Claudia Gabel, thanks for stepping in and offering notes and insight.

Jess MacLeish, I am so grateful for your careful, precise, excellent editing and feedback on this story.

Ben Rosenthal, thank you for guiding *Fortune Tellers* from a very rough draft to a finished book.

To the superstars of the HarperCollins team: Molly Fehr, Joel Tippie, Kristen Eckhardt, Jon Howard, Gwen Morton, Anna Ravanelle, Sabrina Aballe, Patty Rosati, and Mimi Rankin: you're all phenomenal and I am so grateful to be part of this community.

Caroline Hickey and Lisa Graff: nearly twenty years of laughs, friendship, and writing retreats—it's unbelievable. I am so lucky to have the two of you in my life.